Pink & Green

IS THE

NEW BLACK

Pink & Green

LISA GREENWALD

IS THE
NEW BLACK

AMULET BOOKS

NEW YORK

Library of Congress Cataloging-in-Publication Data
Greenwald, Lisa.
Pink & green is the new black / Lisa Greenwald.
pages cm. — (Pink & green ; book 3)
ISBN 978-1-4197-1225-8 (hardback) — ISBN 978-1-61312-700-1 (ebook)
[1. Middle schools—Fiction. 2. Schools—Fiction. 3. Cosmetics—Fiction. 4. Dating (Social customs)—Fiction.] I. Title. II. Title: Pink and green is the new black.
PZ7.G85199Pi 2014
[Fic]—dc23
2014011249

Printed and bound in U.S.A.
10 9 8 7 6 5 4 3 2 1

Amulet Books are available at special discounts when purchased in quantity for premiums and promotions as well as fundraising or educational use. Special editions can also be created to specification. For details, contact specialsales@abramsbooks.com or the address below.

ABRAMS
THE ART OF BOOKS SINCE 1949
115 West 18th Street
New York, NY 10011
www.abramsbooks.com

For Alyssa Eisner Henkin, who mentioned makers and spas on a phone call many years ago

My dad and I are sitting on the rocking chairs on the front porch drinking hot chocolate. It's freezing outside, but sometimes you need fresh air, even in January.

"Are you sure this is instant hot chocolate?" my dad asks. "It tastes like gourmet, like the homemade kind they have at 384 Sprinkles."

I know he's just saying this to be nice. It's nothing fancy, just the powdered kind, but to me it's delicious. My dad doesn't live with us, but he's close enough that he's able to stop by pretty much every other day. It's so much better than when he lived in London. Every visit with my dad needed careful planning and of course involved plane tickets and school breaks and passports. Now we can have hot chocolate in the middle of the week, whenever we feel like it, without really even having to plan. It's pretty great.

"Are you okay, Luce? You seem quiet."

I nod. "Yeah, I'm fine."

Once you start telling people you're fine and that nothing is wrong, it's hard to go back and say that there is actually something bothering you. I've gotten so used to saying everything is fine that it just kind of comes out of my mouth now. A tiny part of me even believes it.

And the thing is, so many parts of my life really are great. Our family's eco-spa is up and running, and business is booming. Grandma is so happy about that, and Mom is too. They barely fight these days. Dad lives close by and I see him all the time. Sunny and I are BFFs like always, and in a way it seems like we've gotten even closer. All my efforts at the pharmacy and on the grant totally paid off, and my work with Earth Club has been going well too. The school board vote on approving a green cafeteria is tomorrow night.

But even when so many things are going well, there can still be lingering frustrating parts to life. And sometimes, even if you don't talk about them, those things take over.

"You'd tell me if something was wrong, right?" my dad asks, finishing the last few sips of hot chocolate.

I nod again but don't say anything. It's not like something is seriously wrong—not like I'm failing out of school or I robbed a bank or anything. If things were really bad, I could talk about it. At least I think I could. But right now all my thoughts are jumbled like a word search. It's hard to express your feelings when you're not even sure how you feel.

Our hands are about to freeze, so we head inside and put our mugs in the dishwasher. Grandma is making her famous chicken potpie for dinner, and Mom is closing up at the pharmacy.

"You staying for dinner, Sam?" Grandma asks from the stove.

"Um, sure, I'd love to."

I'm grateful for the little things like this.

"Grandma, don't forget that tomorrow is my big meeting with the school board," I tell her. "So I won't be home for dinner."

My grandma is a big believer in the whole family-eating-together thing. Claudia's back at school, so it's just the three of us again. Except when Dad stays for dinner, and then it's the four of us.

"Got it, Lucy. You all set for that?" She finally turns around and faces me. "Any last-minute preparations?"

"I don't think so." I pop a grape in my mouth. "We've been ready for ages, since we were supposed to have the meeting in October. Waiting for the school board to put it back on the agenda after the hurricane hasn't fazed us at all."

"She talks like an adult, doesn't she, Sam?" My grandma laughs. "Thirteen going on forty-five."

I want to tell her that there's an actual movie called *13 Going on 30*, but I don't because I get what she's saying. Most kids wouldn't really care that much about a school board meeting, but I've been working on making the cafeteria green since last year. It may actually happen soon. Fingers crossed.

My dad has to make a few calls for work, and Grandma is busy finishing dinner. My homework is done, so I go upstairs to check my e-mail.

But as soon as I sign in, I see that there's nothing new. I had hoped that Yamir would get in touch, but both my phone and e-mail are just as I left them this morning.

I can't be the one to contact him again. It just makes me feel stupid. But sitting here thinking all of this makes me feel stupid too.

The one good thing is that Yamir is my best friend's brother, so I can always call their house, looking for Sunny— but really hoping Yamir picks up the phone. The only problem is that I rarely call their home phone anymore, now that we all have cell phones. I wonder why anyone even bothers having a landline.

"I tried your cell but it went straight to voice mail," I say to Sunny after she answers. I'm totally lying and she probably knows it, but that's the thing about best friends—sometimes it's okay to tell a little lie.

"Oh, my battery's probably dead again," she says. "What's up?"

I listen very carefully to see if I can hear Yamir in the background. If he's home and didn't e-mail or text, that will be even more upsetting. But it sounds like he's still out, at basketball practice maybe.

"Oh, nothing. Just bored. Did you understand the math homework?" As I talk, I keep refreshing my e-mail in-box. But still nothing.

"Kind of. Those word problems are always hard," she says. "But Mrs. O'Rourke never minds explaining it the next day if we're confused."

It seems like Sunny's home alone, because it's silent in her house. "So, what are you doing now?"

"Just sitting around. My dad has a meeting tonight, so my mom said we were going out for Mexican food, but now it's snowing again."

"It is?" I ask, even though I can easily turn my head and look out the window. "Oh, weird."

Please say where Yamir is. Please say where Yamir is. I don't want to have to ask. I wish Sunny would know that I need this information. She is my best friend, after all.

"Just you and your mom are going out for dinner?" I know I'm being obvious, but I don't even care. It's gotten to that point.

"Well, Yamir was supposed to come, but I think he went to some kid's house after basketball, and I'm not sure when he's getting back." She groans. "Anyway, what's new with you?"

"Nada. Just trying to make sure everything is done before tomorrow's meeting. Did Mrs. Deleccio tell you when we're going up to speak?"

"Lucy, you were at the same meeting I was, and she said she doesn't know the order yet," Sunny tells me, like I'm totally out of it. "Are you okay? You seem all weird."

If both Sunny and my dad are asking if I'm okay, I guess I need to work on my acting skills. I don't want to be the girl who's all consumed over a guy. It's embarrassing, especially because I don't even know if there's really anything to be upset about.

It's just that it seemed like things were great and then one day they weren't. I guess the change didn't happen over a single day, more like over time. It's hard to say when, exactly. But after a while, I realized something was wrong.

So of course I'm going to feel confused. And now all I can think about is making it all great again. I can't accept that this weird, not-knowing feeling is just the way things are now.

"Yeah. I'm fine. I'm just nervous about the meeting."

Sunny laughs. "Lucy! Come on, you'll be fine. I'm sure they already okayed the whole thing and are just making us speak to impress all the parents." She pauses for a second, and I listen extra hard for Yamir. "They're not going to say no to a green cafeteria. It's the right thing to do. Especially after all the work we put into it."

"You're right," I say, because I don't really feel like talking about this anymore. "Anyway, I gotta go set the table. Enjoy your Mexican food. Pancho's or Enchiladas?"

"Pancho's, I think," Sunny says. "My mom thinks it's *soooo* much better, even though she only eats cheese quesadillas."

I laugh. Her mom really isn't an adventurous eater.

"I gotta go, Luce. My mom is calling me. Smooches."

She hangs up, and I realize I don't have any more information than I had before I called.

Why is Yamir ignoring me?

I think his ignoring me means something more than just being busy. Something way worse.

Lucy's tip for surviving eighth grade:
It's okay to change your mind about things.

Yamir doesn't call or text or anything to wish me good luck before the school board meeting. Maybe I shouldn't expect him to. I mean, he's in high school now, and the Old Mill Middle School Earth Club isn't part of his life anymore. But still, it would have been nice.

I'm sick of feeling like this, though—always wondering when I will hear from him. And besides, I have too many awesome things to focus on.

On my way into school, I decide to have a new outlook: I'm not going to stress over boys anymore. It's my last semester of middle school, and I need to make it the absolute best it can be. I'll never be here, in this place, with these people again. I need to make it count.

I need to make it perfect.

"Hey, Luce," Annabelle Wilson says. She's at her locker,

reorganizing for the millionth time. She must have the neatest locker in the whole school. "Ready for tonight? I even brought a new dress to wear, in case we don't have time to go home and change."

"That was such a good idea. I guess I'll just have my mom or grandma bring over a dress." I close my locker and sit down on the floor for a few minutes before the first bell rings.

"Can you believe the meeting is tonight?" Annabelle asks.

"Not really. But kind of. If that makes any sense." What I really can't believe is that Annabelle and I are friends now. In seventh grade we just worked together in Earth Club. And then last summer she took Bevin under her wing. But since the beginning of the year, we've actually become friends. I've even been to her house a few times. She's a kiss-up, but I don't mind it as much anymore. Sometimes she can be fun.

"We're going to be awesome." Annabelle high-fives me. "See you at Earth Club later."

Even though Annabelle and I are both in honors classes, we're in different sections, so we never see each other throughout the day. Maybe that's why it's easy for us to be friends. We have so much to talk about when we do see each other. I guess I can look at the Yamir situation that way too. We may not be seeing much of each other, but that means we should have tons to talk about, different experiences to share.

Only we can't share them, since he never calls! It's maddening.

Also, I think it's different with a boyfriend. I think you're supposed to hang out a lot. I could be wrong, but I'm pretty sure I'm right. Sunny and Evan hang out all the time. Same with my sister, Claudia, and her boyfriend, Bean. If you're in a relationship, you should spend time together. That's just the way it is. Otherwise what's the point of being in the relationship?

Sunny runs into school four seconds before the first bell rings. She's out of breath and she's rolling her bag on the floor instead of carrying it over her shoulder. It's the kind of backpack that can be carried both ways.

I'm putting some finishing touches on my "school day" makeup application, using the magnetic pink mirror that I keep inside my locker. I'm not really allowed to wear a lot of makeup to school, but I always do a quick mineral powder spread to make sure my skin looks even, a drop of pale pink eye shadow, and some clear lip gloss.

It helps me feel ready for the day. More awake. More put together.

And when I've had a stressful morning, a quick makeup application relaxes me. It helps me to slow down and focus.

"Mrs. O'Rourke is going to kill me. Again." Sunny throws a few textbooks on the top shelf of her locker and slams the door. "I'm always late to her class."

"She does hate tardiness," I say, which I realize isn't helpful after I say it. "And I do too. I have a stomachache just thinking about it. Come on."

"Calm down," Sunny says, rolling her eyes. She straightens out her sweater. "Okay, I'm ready. Let's go."

"Why are you late?" I ask. I know that's probably not a question Sunny wants to answer, but best friends want to know everything.

"Well, I overslept. Yamir took seventeen years in the bathroom, and then I had to shower. I burnt my toast, and my dad was on a business call when he was supposed to drive me." She takes a banana out of her bag. "And now I'm starving, so I'm eating in the hallway and I don't even care."

There's a "no eating except in the cafeteria" rule, but no one really follows it, especially the eighth graders. We're pretty good at sneaking food with no one seeing.

"Sounds like a hectic morning," I say. We get to Mrs. O'Rourke's math class with a minute to spare and take our seats. Georgina and Eve are already working on the Problem of the Day like they're going to win a prize for figuring it out first. Annabelle has turned them into overachievers. They're not quite at her level yet, but they're getting close.

I try to pay attention in class, but all I can think about is tonight's meeting. Every time the Yamir thing pops into my thoughts, I force myself to focus on the meeting instead. I have much more control over the meeting. I've done the prep work and I know what I'm going to say. I can do my best to bring about the outcome I want.

With Yamir, it's not like that at all. It sometimes seems like there's nothing I can do to make it the way I want it to be. And it's messing up my plan to have a perfect end to middle school.

At lunch, everyone is already at our table when I get there. I put down my bag and go to wait in the salad bar line.

Most people don't spend so much time thinking about their school cafeteria. But it's been on my mind so much these past few years that it's become a major part of my life. I see the plastic trays and imagine the biodegradable ones I found from the supplier. I see the plastic utensils and imagine switching to reusable metal ones. It's a great idea. The school board has to say yes.

When I get back to the table, it's clear that everyone has been whispering about me. I don't think there's anything more awkward than that. I never know if I should pretend I don't notice or just ask them what they were saying. I decide to sit there and put the ranch dressing on my salad, sip my iced tea, and stay quiet. These are my friends, so they probably weren't saying anything bad.

But they keep staring at me as I chew a cucumber, and then it starts to get really weird.

"What?" I laugh. "Do I have a stain on my shirt or something?"

"No." Eve shakes her head. "Nothing like that. I was just saying how lucky you are that you have an actual, real boyfriend who is in high school."

Eve is definitely the most boy-crazy one at the table. She thinks everything should be the way it is in movies. She steals romance novels from her mom's bookshelf and loves to hear stories about how people propose and get engaged. It's kind of her hobby.

My cheeks get hot and I look at Sunny. She lives with Yamir—she has to know the truth, that my boyfriend isn't so much of a boyfriend anymore. I barely even see him. But she stays quiet, smiles and nods, and takes a bite out of her turkey wrap.

"Oh." I shrug. "Yeah, I guess. I mean, it's just Yamir."

"Just Yamir?" Georgina shrieks. "Okay, I know he's Sunny's brother and I don't want to gross her out, but he was the cutest kid in eighth grade last year!"

Georgina is a close second in the boy-crazy department. She's, like, Eve's sidekick for everything. So if Eve is into something, Georgina is too. But I think it's more that she wants to make Eve feel like she's not the only boy-crazy one. Georgina's one of those people who will always tell you you're doing the right thing. If you ever need any positive reinforcement, talk to Georgina.

"Grossing me out. Thanks." Sunny looks down at the tinfoil around her sandwich. "Cool if you stop now."

"He's in high school. That's all I'm saying," Eve adds, but then continues—so it clearly wasn't all she was saying. "He's in a whole different school and he still chooses to be your boyfriend. That's a big deal."

"We're going to be in high school next year too," I remind them. "But thanks. It's cool to feel cool." I laugh at how stupid that sounds and try to think of a way to change the topic.

"Speaking of boyfriends, where's Evan?" Eve asks Sunny. I think Eve keeps some kind of checklist on boyfriends—who has one, where they are, what they're doing. She keeps saying she prays every night that we'll all have one by Eighth-Grade Masquerade. We only have a couple of months to make that happen, and I'm not sure Annabelle even talks to boys except when it's about Earth Club or Mathletes.

"He only sits with us on Fridays." Sunny laughs. "You know that."

It's true, but it's funny when she says it out loud like it's an actual rule. At the beginning of the year, Sunny wanted Evan to sit with her at lunch, but Evan also wanted to sit with his friends. So they made up this silly plan that Evan would sit at our table on Fridays and Sunny would sit at his table on Mondays. But Sunny still sits at our table all the time, and Friday is pizza day anyway, so most people just grab slices and sit wherever they feel like.

It seems like their relationship is always perfect. I don't know what they're doing that I can't do. Maybe Sunny can teach a class on how to have a successful relationship. Or forget the class—maybe she can just teach me. Best friends are supposed to help each other out with those kinds of things.

"*Riiiight.*" Eve laughs. "I forgot." As much as Annabelle has grown on me, Eve still bugs me. I guess everyone can't be perfect.

So we spend the rest of lunch talking about who in the grade has boyfriends and who doesn't, and who is going to bring a date to Eighth-Grade Masquerade. The conversation is making my stomach hurt, and I can barely finish my salad.

"Sunny and Lucy are so lucky that they don't have to worry

about this," Georgina says. "If I can make Harrison Tate know my name by the dance, I'll consider myself lucky."

"Georgina!" I shout, too loud for the cafeteria. Mr. Mikros gives me a look. "Don't be so hard on yourself. He's new to the school. I bet he doesn't know anyone's name."

"He knows *my* name," Eve says. "His dad just fixed our sprinklers and Harrison came to help him, and it was *soooo* embarrassing."

"He went to your house and you didn't even tell me?" Georgina squeals. "That's, like, against every code of friendship. You should have been texting me as soon as you saw his dad's truck roll into your driveway."

"He didn't come in a truck," Eve says, completely serious.

Georgina rolls her eyes. "You know what I mean."

Thankfully, the bell rings just in time, and we can end this silly discussion. Only five more periods and then school is over. After that, the Earth Club prep meeting, and then the meeting I've been waiting months for will finally be here.

Work hard on things that are important to you.

Sunny meets me at our lockers after the final bell rings. We don't have eighth period together, since four days a week she takes French and I take Spanish, and once a week we're in different art electives.

"Mrs. Deleccio said to meet her outside her office," Sunny says.

"Okay." I throw my books in my locker and take a pen and a notebook with me. "Hopefully I'll have time to ask Mom or Grandma to bring a dress over. Annabelle was smart and brought one with her, but I totally forgot."

"My mom can bring an extra for you," Sunny says. "She has to drive right by here anyway on her way to pick Yamir up from swimming."

"Swimming? In January?"

"Yeah, he's trying out for the swim team. So he practices

some afternoons." She looks at me crookedly. "Wait. You didn't know that?"

"Oh, um, I think I did. I just spaced. I'm so nervous for tonight, y'know."

She doesn't believe me. "Lucy. Come on." We stop walking and she puts a hand on my shoulder. "Let's talk for a second. We don't have to meet Mrs. Deleccio until 3:45."

We sit down on the big blocks in the lobby. It's kind of an unofficial student lounge, since we don't have a student lounge.

"So, what's up?" Sunny asks, giving me her most sympathetic smile.

"I don't really know. I guess that's the problem."

"Well, what don't you know?"

"Over Christmas break Yamir and I saw each other every day. Remember? But since then, he's basically been ignoring me. I thought it was because basketball started, but maybe it's something else. I don't know what to do."

"Just ask him," Sunny says, like it's the easiest thing in the world.

"I don't want him to know I care that much."

"Huh? That doesn't make sense."

"I can't explain it."

We sit there for a few more minutes going back and forth,

not getting anywhere, and then it's time to meet Mrs. Deleccio. We're almost at her office when Sunny says, "I know what's bugging you. That everyone thinks it's so perfect. And that you know it's not exactly the way it seems."

"That might be part of it. I really want everything to be perfect."

"Well, everyone doesn't need to know everything. You know?"

It sort of feels like we're speaking in code right now, but that's one of the amazing things about having a real, true best friend. You can speak in code and know exactly what the other is saying without even trying that hard to decipher it.

"I guess. But isn't that like lying?" I say quietly, almost in a whisper.

"Not so much. More like just being a private person." Sunny smiles. "Trust me. I've got your back."

Everyone needs a best friend like Sunny. Sure, we've had our ups and downs, but it's really been more up than down. And when you have a friend like that, even scary things aren't as scary as they would be alone.

"I don't even know what you see in him, honestly," Sunny says as we finish our conversation outside the middle school faculty offices.

"That's because he's your brother," I explain.

"So tell me what's so great about him as a boyfriend. Tell me three things."

I hesitate for a second, wondering if this is something I can even put into words. And I especially don't know if I can do it on the spot.

"Well, he's easy to talk to. I feel like he gets me. Like, sometimes he knows what I'm about to say before I even say it. And he's funny; he always makes me laugh. And I never get bored of him. I'm always excited to see him."

"That may have been more than three things." Sunny squints. "I lost count. But good answers. Let's continue this conversation later, when no one else is around."

I nod in agreement.

The door to Mrs. Deleccio's office is open a little, so we knock softly and walk in.

"Welcome, ladies," Mrs. Deleccio says. In all my time at Old Mill Middle School, I've never been in her office, and it feels special. She arranged some chairs in a circle and put out mini doughnuts and cups of water. This feels like the most official, grown-up Earth Club meeting we've ever had. Annabelle and Evan are already there. Our Greening the Cafeteria Committee is complete.

"Any questions? Additions? Concerns?" Mrs. Deleccio asks. She's wearing a wool sweater with embroidered pens, pencils, blackboards, and chalk on it. I'm pretty sure a student made it, since one sleeve is longer than the other and the collar droops. But she wears it anyway. That's the kind of teacher she is.

"Will they give us their decision tonight?" Evan asks.

"Most likely," Mrs. Deleccio says. "There are a few other proposals up before yours. One about the parking lot, another about temporary classrooms. Boring stuff." She laughs. "And then you guys. You're all going up together?"

I nod. "We know the order. We decided that alphabetical by first name made sense. So Annabelle, Evan, me, Sunny."

"Sounds great. I'll be sitting there cheering you guys on, and available for any last-minute questions."

After the meeting, Annabelle goes to get help from her math teacher. She doesn't really need help, but she does it anyway. Evan decides he's going to shoot hoops with whoever is in the gym, so Sunny and I call her mom and decide to go back to her house for a little while before the meeting.

"Which dress do you want to borrow?" she asks.

I think about it for a second. "Maybe that green sweater one you got on sale a few weeks ago. And can I borrow tights too?"

"Of course."

As soon as I see Sunny's mom's car pulling into the school

parking lot, my heart starts pounding. If Yamir is sitting in the front seat, I won't know what to say. I wonder if he even realizes he's been ignoring me. Sometimes boys are oblivious to that stuff. He could think that everything is perfectly fine, for all I know.

But he's not in the front seat. I don't know if I'm relieved or disappointed. Sunny hops in front. I sit in back, staring out the window and telling myself that everything will be okay.

I wonder if I cared about him this much when things were fine between us. Sometimes life is weird like that. You only obsess over something when it's gone sour. Why don't we ever get excited about the good things?

"Where's Yamir?" Sunny asks, and I bet she's doing that just for me. She doesn't care where Yamir is. She probably wouldn't even mind if he moved to India to live with their grandma.

"Something about studying with Anthony," Mrs. Ramal says, sounding suspicious. "I guess we'll find out if he was telling the truth when his report card comes."

Sunny groans. "Yeah, right. If he gets anything above a C, I'll pass out from shock."

"Sunita, enough." Mrs. Ramal turns down the Indian music and glances at me in the backseat. "Lucy, my darling, how are you?"

I've always loved the way Mrs. Ramal calls me "my darling." She pretty much calls everyone that, but it still feels special.

"Pretty good. Excited that the meeting is tonight. Then we have to start getting ready for Eighth-Grade Masquerade."

I could have just stopped at "pretty good." I don't know why I went into an explanation. I wonder if she can tell that I'm really trying to act calm despite the stress her son is causing me.

"Ah yes. The big dance. Exciting!"

Sunny turns around and gives me a look, but for once I can't figure out what she's trying to say. That her mom is weird? That I won't have a date? I decide to ignore it.

Back at Sunny's, we're trying on dresses since we have lots of time. She puts on this pink fluffy thing that she's worn to a million bar and bat mitzvahs.

"Too much," I say. "We need to look professional."

She nods, and slips it off.

I thought I wanted to wear her new green sweater dress, but I've changed my mind a million times after looking through Sunny's closet. Finally I try on her gray A-line dress with the skinny silver belt. "What about this for me?"

"I love it! You can wear my black ballet flats and my houndstooth tights."

"Perfect!" I love wearing Sunny's clothes. It's a miracle that we're both the same size and have the same tastes. It's like we were put on this earth to be best friends. But so many variables could have kept us apart. Her parents could have stayed in India. My parents could have stayed together and moved to the Berkshires, like they used to dream about. Anything could have happened. But the universe wanted us to be BFFs, and so we are.

Sunny puts on her flowing blue maxi dress, even though it's really for summer, and wears a silver cardigan over it. She has silver ballet flats that match perfectly.

"That's the outfit," I tell her. "You look sophisticated and smart."

"Ha! I'll take it!"

Next, we test eye shadow colors.

I'm immediately more relaxed. Kind of like how people feel better once they start running or at the beginning of their yoga class. I put a brush to a face, and I feel better right away.

If this school year continues the way it's been going, I'm probably going to look like I'm in a Broadway show every single day.

I'm trying out this sparkly silver shadow when the phone rings. Her mom yells, "Sunita, answer the phone, please!" from downstairs, but Sunny is mid-eye with the eyeliner pencil, so she tells me to get it.

I've already said "hello" when I realize I should've announced myself.

"Hello?" the voice on the other end says, confused.

"Um, it's Lucy." I sound tentative and scared, my least favorite tone.

"Oh! Luce-Juice!" Yamir sounds excited but normal, like I answer the phone at his house every day, like we just talked an hour ago.

"What's up?"

"Well, first of all, how are you?" He's using that jokey but confident voice that I like so much. To me, it seems like nothing in the world ever bothers him, like everything's always going to be okay, like he has everything under control.

"I'm good." I freeze. Suddenly I can't think of a single thing to say. To Yamir, my boyfriend. If that's what he is.

"Yeah? Good. Good to hear you're good." He pauses for a second too, and then says, "Listen, can you tell *mi madre* that Sir Anthony is giving me a ride home, and that yes, I have my key."

"Anthony drives now?"

He laughs. "Yes, Luce, they changed the driving age to fourteen. Very funny. His *mamacita* is driving us home."

"Got it. I'll tell her."

"Thanks," he says. "Oh, and good luck tonight."

I hang up the phone and I'm all flickery, like fireworks as they're about to fall into the ocean. I can't stop smiling. Nothing even happened. He didn't say where he's been or why he hasn't called. But he did say good luck. He remembered. Sometimes remembering is the most important thing of all.

Lucy's tip for surviving eighth grade:
Try to act confident even when you're not
feeling that way.

Ꮥunny's mom drives us back to school, and all I can see are Yamir's muddy sneakers on the floor in the backseat. I didn't notice them before, but now I do. Something about them being here makes me happy. It's strange, though—who leaves sneakers in the car? Did he walk into the house barefoot?

"Good luck, darlings," Mrs. Ramal says, and then we walk inside. It always feels funny to be at school after hours, when it's dark out. It almost makes school seem more exciting, like I'd be able to pay attention better if we went to class at night. Even the ugly peach wall tiles look pretty when I see them at night.

"Ready?" Sunny squeezes my hand as we walk into the auditorium. There's a table set up on the stage, and people are already filling out the seats in the audience. It's hard to believe that so many came out on a freezing-cold winter night. They must really care about the schools.

"They pay taxes. They want to know what's going on," Sunny explains. I bet she's repeating something her dad said once, but it sounds smart.

Annabelle and Evan are up front, by the stage, chatting with Mrs. Deleccio. Evan and Sunny high-five when they see each other, which I think is pretty cool. It's not like they're going to smooch in front of anyone.

"Why don't you guys sit over here, and then we'll all go up together when they call us?" Mrs. Deleccio guides us to a row of seats toward the front.

Suddenly it all feels real. I'm wearing a whole outfit of Sunny's and it's snowing outside and we're in school at night and we're about to make our presentation. In a way, I realize I've been waiting forever for this, and in another way, I find it hard to believe that it's actually here.

This is all part of the end of middle school—a time that I'll remember forever. It has to go right, and I'm confident it will. But it's more than nerves I'm feeling. I really need it to be perfect. I'm only going to do this once; there's no do-over. I don't want to constantly think about what I could have done differently, if only I had the chance.

But life is like that too. There's no do-over. Maybe we

should approach every situation like this, constantly trying for perfection.

The president of the school board, Clint's dad, goes up to the microphone and starts the meeting. I zone out for the beginning part, since it's pretty boring to discuss the sizes of the parking spots in the high school student lot. Then there's some discussion about adding an extra position for a technology teacher in the elementary school, which is borderline interesting. Next is a big debate about adding temporary classrooms on the field behind the elementary school to make room for students with special needs. People get heated over this one, but I can't figure out why. The more the merrier, right?

Finally it's our turn.

"Next on the agenda is our big presentation from the Old Mill Middle School Earth Club," Clint's dad says. "I'd like to call up Lucy Desberg, Evan Mass, Sunita Ramal, and Annabelle Wilson."

I crack up when he says Sunita, because he stumbles over it a little bit and then gets all embarrassed. I don't know why; he's a lawyer, so he must talk in front of people all the time.

Annabelle goes to the microphone first, just like we planned. "Hello, everyone. Welcome, and thanks for coming out on this freezing night." I'm really impressed with how she speaks. She kind of sounds like my rabbi, composed and smiley. "We've been working on this proposal since last year, and we're so excited about it. We know it will make a huge difference in our school and help the environment." She looks down at her notes and back at us sitting in the folding chairs behind her—and then everything goes downhill. It's like she's completely forgotten why she's there and what she's supposed to say. She's quiet for only a few seconds, but it seems like a million years. "Um, I . . . Um." She looks back at us, and I nod, and then she says, finally, "I'd like to introduce Lucy Desberg. Um, this was all her idea, and she will, um, go into the specific details."

I look around. Evan was supposed to go next, but maybe Annabelle forgot that too. I stand up and straighten out my dress and walk over to the podium.

I smile at Annabelle so she won't feel completely terrible. The audience looks so serious. Or maybe they're bored and just want to get home. It's hard to say. I take my place behind the microphone and smile at no one in particular.

"Hi, everyone. I'm Lucy Desberg. Nice to see you." I glance down at my note cards. My hands are sweaty and they're crinkling the paper. I try to stand up straight, speak slowly, and smile. "When I first joined Earth Club, I had no idea what I was getting into. I thought it would be fun, and

I wanted the free snacks." I pause for some laughter, hoping that people find it funny. Thankfully, they do. "But after a few meetings, I became passionate about helping the environment. Thinking of ways to go green literally kept me up at night. And I discovered that one of the main areas we could improve was a place we visited every day: the school cafeteria. Until now we have been using plastic utensils, plastic trays, and Styrofoam cups. Many of our snacks are prepackaged, and we don't eat locally grown fruits and vegetables. All of this can be fixed, and pretty easily too." I pause and smile and look out at the audience. They seem to be paying attention, and no one has fallen asleep yet. "So I'd like to introduce a fellow Earth Club member, Evan Mass, who will go over all the suppliers we've researched, and Sunny—I mean, Sunita—Ramal will talk about the budget for this plan. And of course, we'll have time for questions at the end."

"Fab job, Lulu," Evan whispers, and slaps me a low five. He's wearing khakis that are a tiny bit too short and a wrinkly blue button-down. He looks like a little boy. But he's Evan. Steady, reliable, funny Evan.

When Evan's up at the podium, I turn to Sunny and whisper, "He's great."

She nods. "I know. Also, you rocked out there. You totally

saved Annabelle and didn't even make it seem too obvious."

Sunny finishes up by going over the costs and asking if anyone has questions.

Of course people have questions. This is Old Mill. And as my sixth-grade science teacher, Mrs. Kurtz, said, "Thinking people ask questions."

"Where did you find these suppliers?" one man asks, so I go to the microphone and tell him all about our research.

"What's the timetable for this kind of change?" a woman wants to know. I start, and Mrs. Deleccio finishes up that one.

A short man sitting in the front row says, "This is a question specifically for Lucy." He pauses for a second, as if making sure he has the room's attention. "How did you get started with this project? Can you talk a little about your inspiration for this kind of work?"

I stand up near my seat and answer. "My friend Sunny is actually the main reason." I look over at her. I explain how she encouraged me to join Earth Club. And then I talk a little about the spa and the grant and all that. "But the cafeteria project was my baby," I say. "There was just so much waste. I knew we could do better. I wanted to help us do better."

"Thank you," the man says, and a few people applaud. It's weak applause, but it's still something.

Finally the questions end, and Clint's dad tells us they

should have a decision within the next few days. "We are so impressed with the work you've done," he says. "This is a testament to the fabulous school district that we're so lucky to be a part of. Under the direction of Susan Deleccio, this club can save the world."

He's a little cheesy, but I like what he's saying. Mrs. Deleccio suggests that we all go to 384 Sprinkles for dessert, and of course no one can say no to that. It may be January, but ice cream is a year-round food, if you ask me.

Sunny and I share the Sprinkles Explosion—five scoops of ice cream and five toppings. It's a little much, but this is a celebration, after all.

"Congrats, guys," Mrs. Deleccio says. "I'm so impressed. Now all we can do is wait. But I have a feeling the wait won't be too long."

That night as I'm falling asleep, I can't help but feel grateful. The meeting went well, Yamir remembered to wish me good luck, and we got ice cream afterward.

To me, that's a pretty perfect day.

Lucy's tip for surviving eighth grade:

Be patient.

I wait and wait for an answer from the school board, even though I don't even know how they're going to get in touch. They could e-mail it, or real-mail it, or just send Mrs. Deleccio some kind of teacher memo. I have no idea.

But Friday afternoon rolls around and there's still no answer. I guess it takes time.

"What are we doing this weekend?" Sunny asks me after school.

"You tell me," I say. "You always come up with the better ideas."

"I'll tell you what we're doing," Erica Crane says, plopping herself down on the bench next to me. "We're starting the prep for Eighth-Grade Masquerade. And you, Lucy Desberg, are joining the team."

"Huh?" Sunny asks, taking the word right out of my mouth.

"We need you, Lucy."

"I'll explain," Zoe says, jumping into the conversation. Zoe's new this year, and she's been Erica's sidekick since her first day at Old Mill. She moved from Long Island, so Erica thinks she's fancy, and Zoe finds Erica completely hilarious.

They're a match made in heaven.

"You're the makeup guru, right?" Zoe asks.

This is the most she's said to me all year. How does she know I'm the makeup guru?

I shrug. "I guess."

"Come on, Lucy. Of course you are." Sunny rolls her eyes.

"Anyway, so Erica and I are on the planning committee for student council, and we would like to bring you on as our makeup consultant," Zoe says. "Sunny, you can come on too. Maybe help with publicity?"

I look at Erica and Zoe, and then at Sunny. Erica and Zoe never talk to us, but now they seem to have a whole plan laid out. It feels like they're recruiting us for some secret mission.

"Sounds good to me," Sunny says. "We need another extracurricular, Lucy."

"We do?" I ask. Is this really my best friend Sunny talking?

"Sure. Why not? And the school board proposal is pretty much over. What else are we going to do?"

I nod. I guess she's right. I hadn't thought about that, and suddenly I feel all anxious to start planning. I love having projects! Plus, if I don't have something to do, I might end up spending all my time worrying about Yamir.

"Great, then it's settled," Erica says. "Lucy, we're going to need a pre-event visit at your spa. Okay? Talk to my assistant to set that up."

"Your assistant?"

She nods. "Yeah, Zoe Feldman. She's right here."

"You're Erica's assistant?" I ask, but she's too busy typing something into her phone to notice.

Finally our bus comes and we say good-bye to Erica and Zoe. It almost feels like what just happened is some kind of weird dream. I guess it's good to be wanted, though. And that's probably the nicest Erica has been to me since kindergarten. Maybe Zoe is a good influence on her.

"It'll be fun," Sunny says when we're on the bus. "I mean, we might as well get involved. We're only going to have one Eighth-Grade Masquerade."

"You're so right, and that's totally how I've been feeling lately," I tell her.

"Explain?"

"That we're only going to be in our last semester of middle school once. And we have to make it awesome. Actually, more than awesome. We have to make it perfect," I explain.

She looks at me. "Yeah, but—"

"No buts," I say. "We have to."

When we get to my house, my parents are in the kitchen drinking coffee.

"Hey, Luce. Hey, Sunny," my mom calls to us. "Happy weekend."

"Hey," I say back, and Sunny and I go upstairs.

"Is that weird?" Sunny asks when we're in my room with the door closed. "I mean, having your dad around so much? I know it's been like this since the summer, but still."

"Nah." I throw my backpack under my desk. "It's nice. Just little things, like how he helped me with the math homework the other night. Video-chatting on the computer is great and everything, but it's much better to go over complicated problems side by side at the kitchen table. I feel really lucky that he's around."

"That's so great," Sunny says. "Especially since your dad is really good at math."

I run downstairs to grab us some snacks, and when I get back Sunny squeals, "Oh my God, did you see this picture Claudia posted online?" She's on my bed using my laptop. I run over to see what it is, and there's a picture of Claudia and Bean smooching in front of some fountain.

"They're really in love," I say. I didn't like Bean much at

the beginning, but I kind of love him now. He's a part of the family, and even though I won't see him for a while, I can't really imagine things without him.

"They're totally gonna get married, right?" Sunny asks. "How cool is that? They're on their own, in college, in love. It's like a dream."

It's hard to be jealous of my sister, since I'm so happy for her. And also I kind of feel like things will work out for me one day too. When I'm older. I bet I'll have a cool boyfriend when I'm in college.

"Do you think Evan and I will go to college together?" Sunny asks.

"I think it's too soon to tell. You guys have all of high school to get through."

"That's true."

"So, what should we do tonight?" I ask. "Annabelle said something about going to see that movie about the magician. But I'm not sure I feel like it. There's always Friday night rec, but we just went last week."

"Yeah, but we can go again."

Friday night recreation is an Old Mill tradition. I guess parents were worried their kids would become delinquents, so they had the teachers open the middle school to let kids hang out there. Some play basketball and others just sit around chatting.

There's usually pizza and chips and soda. It's pretty fun, actually.

"Ask Evan if he's going," I say.

Last summer I was all annoyed that Evan and Sunny spent so much time together, but for some reason it doesn't bother me as much anymore. It feels like Evan is just another friend now. They're really good at balancing their time together and their time with their friends. It's admirable—but also kind of frustrating, since I seem to be failing at my own relationship.

"Okay, I'll call later. He has tennis after school."

Sunny knows his whole schedule, like they're some kind of married couple.

I go downstairs to get more snacks, and then Sunny tells me I have a text message.

I immediately hope it's from Yamir, even though I've been feeling better about things since our accidental phone call. He wished me luck, and as sad as it sounds, I can live on that for a while.

"It's Erica," Sunny says, rolling her eyes.

"Erica?" I look at my phone.

Wondering if we can check out the spa tonight to start preparing. Zoe, me, you, and Sunny. Let me know.

"So, let's go," Sunny says. "We don't have anything else to do."

"I have to ask my mom and grandma. There may be an event tonight."

Sunny says, "You used to know everything that went on there. You're totally slacking."

I hit her gently on the arm. "Ha-ha. I'm not slacking. I'm just in school, and they have staff to take care of things. I did my job, and now I can relax."

"Okay, so text her back. This is gonna be fun."

I don't know about fun, but I guess it can't hurt. Unless Erica is trying to trick us or humiliate us. But I think she's moved on from her silly pranks. She seems really serious.

I call Grandma at the pharmacy, and she tells me it's fine as long as we don't disturb the customers. This is a change too. Normally she'd make sure she or Mom was there with me, but I guess she trusts me more these days. She knows I can handle it. Plus, Charise is working the pharmacy counter until nine o'clock, and there will be a few people doing late spa treatments. It's not like we'll be totally alone.

Erica and I text back and forth, and we agree to meet there at seven. I tell her that we can only stay an hour. Truthfully, we're allowed to stay until closing at nine, but I don't want to commit to that many hours with Erica Crane.

Improvements or not.

Lucy's tip for surviving eighth grade:
Be open to new ideas.

My dad drives Sunny and me over to the pharmacy, and he keeps asking us questions. "Are you sure this is a good idea, Lucy?"

"Dad, it's for school."

"But Erica Crane? Isn't she a troublemaker? I should've saved all the e-mails you've written me about her."

"People change, Dad." Okay, that may be true, but I doubt it's true in Erica's case. She's still mean and competitive. But I don't need to tell my dad about that, because I know her well enough to know she's not being mean. Not yet, anyway.

Still, I get why he's asking these questions. I'm a little bit worried myself. I try to play it cool, though, and give her the benefit of the doubt.

We pull into the parking lot and Dad says, "Well, have a

good time. Good luck." He gives me a kiss on the forehead and high-fives Sunny.

"You have a cool dad," Sunny says. "He's, like, responsible like a dad, but then fun like a kid. It's pretty much the perfect combination."

"Thanks, Sun."

We walk into the spa and it smells delicious, as always—lavender and eucalyptus with traces of vanilla.

"Lucy!" Grace, the spa receptionist, greets Sunny and me like we're celebrities. "What can I do for you beauties?"

"We're actually meeting two girls from school here," I tell her. "We're starting to prepare for the big eighth-grade dance, and I guess they want me to be in charge of makeup."

"Wow. Exciting!"

I'm about to answer when Grace holds up a finger, telling us to wait, as she picks up the phone. Every time I hear someone say, "Good evening, Pink and Green: The Spa at Old Mill Pharmacy," I feel this wave of excitement. It never gets old.

Grace books a spa appointment for the woman on the phone and then turns back to us with a smile. "All right, well, let me know if you need anything."

Sunny and I are early, so we wander through the pharmacy aisles like the good old days, making sure all the Silly Putty packages are in order and the lollipop bowl on the counter is fully stocked.

I turn to Sunny. "Hey, did I tell you that we finally cleaned out the basement?"

Sunny's eyes bulge. "Really? The thing your mom's been talking about for years and years?"

"Yup. Come down and see! Before everyone else gets here."

The basement at the pharmacy was our main storage facility—everything ended up there: old couches, empty boxes, sets of dishes Grandma didn't want, and of course pharmacy supplies. It was always a huge mess. And it was this thing that hung over my mom's head that my grandma had asked her a million times to deal with.

It took forever, but I'm so glad it's done because it looks amazing down here.

"Wow. This is like a whole other place now," Sunny says. "Honestly, we could hang out down here. Get a big-screen TV and stuff."

"I don't know about that," I say. "But come here, check out what we found!"

On the counter toward the back are a zillion old-fashioned pill bottles all lined up. They're brown and they have cork tops, and it's pretty hard to believe that anyone ever used them for medicine.

"I don't get it. What are they?" Sunny asks.

"People used to get their medicine in these! A million years ago! Aren't they cool looking? They've been down here all along and we had no idea."

"Pretty crazy." Sunny looks a little confused, like she's not sure why it's a big deal. She's still going on and on about how we should turn this basement into our official hangout.

"We should go upstairs and wait for them by the spa," I tell Sunny, after it's clear she's not as impressed by the old bottles as I am. "They probably won't know to look for us here."

We go upstairs and Sunny excuses herself to use the bathroom. I sit in the spa waiting area and flip through a magazine. I'm nervous, even though I really shouldn't be. I'm the one in charge here. This is my pharmacy, my spa, and I'm doing Erica a favor by helping with the makeup. But sometimes your brain isn't in control and there's nothing you can do about it.

"Hi, Lucy, sorry we're late," Zoe says, running in. "My parents have CLS."

"CLS?" I ask.

"Chronic Lateness Syndrome. They can't help it." She smirks. Zoe's petite and covered with freckles, and it's clear she thinks she's the cutest person on earth. In a way, she's self-confident and funny and likable, and in another way her whole attitude is kind of annoying. I can't totally decide how I feel about her, but I'm committed to getting to know her better.

"So, before we start," Zoe says, "Erica tells me you have a boyfriend in high school?"

It's a good thing Sunny's in the bathroom, because she always gets grossed out when people talk about her brother that way. And also because she knows the truth. It's hard to keep up a lie when people all around you know the truth.

"Yeah, I do. His name is Yamir." I smile so they don't think I'm full of myself.

"He's super cute," Erica adds. "He was definitely the cutest eighth grader last year."

"Thanks," I say. "I think so too."

"Of course you do." Erica rolls her eyes, and I guess a little bit of her old self is coming back. Despite what I told my dad, Erica Crane can't change completely.

"So, maybe we can all hang out, and then he can introduce me to some of his high school friends?" Zoe asks, all sweet.

"Maybe," I say, and then quickly change my tone. "I mean, sure, yeah."

"Great!" Zoe ties her hair back into a low ponytail. "I really don't know many people here yet, you know. It's January, and I still feel like the new girl."

Thankfully, Sunny gets back from the bathroom, so I don't have to say anything in response to that. Zoe probably doesn't know many people because she only hangs out with Erica. You either love Erica or you hate Erica, and there really isn't much in-between.

"So, should we start?" Sunny asks. "We only have an hour, right?"

"Right." I'm glad Sunny reminded everyone of that. Hours and hours with these two with no end in sight is too much for me to handle.

"By the way," I tell them, "there are people getting treatments right now, so we do have to keep it quiet. But I know that treatment room A is open, so we can go in there, and I can show you the makeup and everything. Sound good?"

"Sounds amazing," Zoe says. "Your family owns this spa?"

I nod.

"Erica, why are you not BFFs with Lucy?" Zoe asks her. "You could be getting free makeovers and massages, like, every day!"

Erica doesn't say anything to that. I bet she wishes her assistant would keep quiet for once.

Mariah, one of the aestheticians, pops her head out of a treatment room. "Let me know if you need anything, okay, Lucy?"

"I can't believe you, like, made this spa," Zoe says, looking at everything as we walk to the treatment room. "Erica was telling me all about it. It's pretty awesome. You have your college essay written already."

I can't help but laugh. "My college essay? I haven't even finished eighth grade yet!"

"I know, I know. My sister just started working on her essay, so my whole family is kind of obsessed with it."

Zoe is still talking about college essays, even though none of us have seriously started thinking about college yet. What I hear Zoe saying is that Erica was actually talking about me, telling Zoe about the spa, and sounding kind of impressed. Sometimes you jump to conclusions about people, assuming what they're thinking, when you really have no idea at all.

"So, what are you guys thinking for the dance?" I sit down and motion for everyone else to do the same.

"You want to talk first or should I?" Zoe asks Erica.

Erica doesn't answer the question but jumps right in. "We want everyone to get their makeup done here, and we'd like you to do it, and we'd like you to offer a discount. Eighth-Grade Masquerade is special because of the awesome costumes and makeup, and you guys are the makeup experts. What you did for Yamir's grade was incredible."

"Lucy can't do everyone's makeup!" Sunny says, way too loud, and I shush her. "She'd have to start, like, tomorrow! The staff has to be able to help her."

Erica glares at me. "Is that true, Lucy? Aren't you the expert?"

"I wouldn't say I'm an expert, but I know what I'm doing." I shift in my seat. I wonder if there will ever come a time when Erica Crane doesn't make me nervous. "Listen, I like to give each client the time and attention they deserve. I can't rush through it. People can make appointments with me on a first-come, first-served basis."

"She really is a professional!" Zoe laughs, and I think I'm starting to like her a little bit more. Sure, she's obsessed with Erica, but she's not afraid of her. That's impressive for someone who's met her so recently.

We're discussing when we should post the sign-up sheet and who else in the spa should do the makeup, so I go out into the reception area and get a pen and a pad to take notes. And who do I see walking right by the spa window?

Yamir. And he's not alone. He's with Clint and Anthony and two girls I don't know.

At first I pretend I don't see them, trying to look like I'm scavenging through the desk for materials. But then I can feel that they've seen me, and how long can a person possibly look through a desk drawer? So I pick my head up and we make eye contact.

Me in the spa reception area at eight on a Friday night, and

Yamir on Ocean Street with his friends and two mystery girls.

I waffle between going out there or just waving from in here and hoping that they leave, but eventually the decision is made for me. Yamir and his people are coming in. Right now.

"Working the late shift, Luce-Juice?" Yamir asks.

"Um, kind of." I fold my arms across my chest, because I don't know what else to do with them. "Erica, Zoe, and Sunny are in back. We're discussing plans for the dance."

"Ah, Eighth-Grade Masquerade. What memories." Clint's being sarcastic, so I ignore him. He's pretty much sarcastic about everything. I'm used to it by now.

"What's that?" one of the girls asks.

"Oh, right. You're new. It's basically just this big dance where people wear costumes. It's kind of like an eighth-grade prom, but better," Yamir says, and I'm surprised he's actually saying that something from eighth grade is cool. He seems so into the high school thing now.

"Fun," she says, but it doesn't sound like she thinks it's fun. She's wearing black leggings and an oversize sweatshirt, and even though that sounds like a sloppy combination, she looks like a model.

"Where are you from?" I ask her. "I'm Lucy, by the way."

"Oh, so *you're* Lucy?" she asks, like she's been hearing about me for years. "I moved from Westport. I'm Sienna."

I make a mental note to ask Sunny about this girl later, but before I realize what's happening, Yamir and his crew are traipsing through the spa, looking into the treatment rooms. They find our group in treatment room A, and soon it feels like there are a thousand people in the spa.

"Is this what they use to clean your pores?" Anthony asks, holding the pumice stone for pedicures.

"No. Don't touch that." I take it away from him.

The longer they stay in here, the more stressed I get. They shouldn't be in here, they definitely shouldn't be touching everything, and I can't be in the same room as Yamir with all these other people. It feels like we're all in a balloon that's about to pop at any second.

"Oh, Yamir—Lucy's boyfriend," I hear Zoe whisper to Erica, and I ignore her, hoping that Yamir doesn't hear her. But it's clear he does—suddenly he starts fiddling with the string on his hooded sweatshirt and making some dumb joke about how he'd like a spa treatment.

Then he's standing in the corner, looking at the wall and admiring the abstract painting of a tree like he's at some kind of fancy art museum. He looks as stressed as I feel.

"Yamir, don't you want to sit next to your girlfriend?" Erica sings. I look down at my feet, but I can feel Sienna staring at me.

"It's okay, guys, I think it's time to go anyway," I announce. "The staff needs to close up."

"Do you want to come with us to Scotty's?" Anthony asks the group, and I have a suspicious feeling that he may have an instant crush on Zoe. It's just a hunch, but my hunches are usually right.

I look at Sunny and Sunny looks at me, and we try to speak with our eyes. I don't want to go to Scotty's. Not with them, anyway. Everyone thinks Yamir is my boyfriend and that everything is great between us, and I just need them to think that for a little while longer. But if we go to Scotty's and he acts weird, or hangs out with Sienna more than he hangs out with me, everyone will know. And by everyone I mean Erica and Zoe.

"Oh, we can't," Sunny says. *Thank God.* "Lucy's coming back to my house and sleeping over, and we have Evan and some of the other guys meeting us there around nine."

Genius. Sunny Ramal: Girl Genius.

"Ooh, Evan and some of the other guys," Clint says. "Well, okay, we're out. Come on, peeps."

And just like that, Yamir and the others walk out of the treatment room and leave the spa.

"It's cool that you and Yamir are together but, like, you can do things apart," Erica says. At first I can't tell if she's being sincere, but then I decide that she is. She's not smirk-ing—that's how I know.

Zoe and Erica totally believe us about the sleepover, and fortunately they don't ask to be invited. Zoe's mom picks them up, and Charise offers to drive Sunny and me home.

"Should I really sleep over?" I ask Sunny.

"Sure. Why not?"

I get to Sunny's and call my mom to tell her I'm sleeping over.

"Lucy, I get worried about this," she says.

"Worried? Why?"

She pauses for a second. "You sleeping over there. While you and Yamir are, I don't know, an item."

I laugh. "Mom, it's fine. I'm hanging out with Sunny."

"Okay," she says, reluctantly. "Please behave."

I don't ask her to elaborate on what she means by that. I don't really want to know. Maybe if I told her what was really going on, she'd realize she doesn't have much to worry about.

I know I'll be up all night thinking about how Yamir is sleeping right there in the next room. I'll be wondering about that girl Sienna, and what exactly she knows about me.

But I'd rather be here than at home, thinking about all of this from five blocks away.

Lucy's tip for surviving eighth grade:
Keep a journal and write down all the
wonderful moments.

𝒯here's one moment that I replay over and over in my head. It happened in October, and sometimes I wonder if I've changed it in my mind, if I remember it differently from the way it actually happened.

I'm not sure.

Yamir and I were sitting at my kitchen table eating grapes. Green ones. My favorite. Well, *eating* may not be the right word. We were throwing them, trying to get them into each other's mouth. It might seem pretty gross to anyone else, but to us it was the best way to eat them.

His hair was longer than it normally was; I guess he needed a haircut. One strand on the right side of his face was hanging into his eye. I remember his eyes vividly. Golden brown, the color of slightly burnt French toast.

He was the Yamir I'd always known. But he was different. He was mine now.

It was an unseasonably warm October day, so we went outside to lie down on the lounge chairs and pretend it was still summer. The pool was closed up but we didn't mind. We soaked up the last remnants of the summer sun. I stayed sideways on my lounge chair and looked at him, and he stayed the same way on his lounge chair and faced me.

And we just stared at each other.

I'm sure we were both thinking the same thing: how perfectly we happy we were.

Lucy's tip for surviving eighth grade:
Spend time with your friends. You need it.

It's hard to know when things changed with Yamir. I look around Sunny's room, trying to figure it out. Sunny has been sleeping for hours while I've been staring at the clock, wondering if Yamir is asleep in his room next door.

It makes me think of souring milk or bread going stale. You don't know exactly when it happens—you just know it happened. But maybe this is different from stale bread or sour milk. Maybe it can be fixed. The bad can be made good. The wrong can be made right. What's done can be undone.

If I just accept that this is how things are, they will never get better. And the next few months will be nowhere close to the perfect I want and need them to be.

I have to keep trying. I have to figure it out.

I roll over and sigh and wish that Sunny would wake up so we could talk. I hate when she falls asleep before me, because then I know I won't be able to fall asleep for hours and hours. It's the way it's always been at our sleepovers.

I guess I finally fall asleep, because an hour or so later I hear a knock on Sunny's door, and it feels like I've been zapped out of a sound sleep.

I wonder if I'm dreaming it. But then I hear another knock, and I hear a whisper through the door. "Luce-Juice."

Yamir.

He's waking me up. But my hair is all disheveled and I probably have morning breath, even though it's not morning. Well, I guess it is. I look at the clock. It's exactly 3:00 A.M.

I get out of bed as silently as possible, trying to make sure the bed frame doesn't creak, and tiptoe to the door.

"Were you awake?" Yamir whispers.

I nod, even though I wasn't. I'm too scared to talk. I don't want my breath to make him pass out.

He takes my hand and leads me down the stairs. It's a good thing everyone in the Ramal family is a heavy sleeper, or they'd probably wake up from all the creaks the stairs make. I swear they have the loudest stairs in the whole world.

"Sorry to wake you," Yamir whispers when we get down-stairs. We sit on the couch, and he turns on the lamp on the end table. His hair is sticking up in weird places and his eyelids are droopy. I wonder if he's been up all night too.

"What's going on?" I ask. I'm still half-asleep, but I keep telling myself that I need to pay attention. Yamir woke me up. He knew I was sleeping here and he wants to talk to me. If I didn't look and feel so discombobulated, this could be really romantic.

"I think you're mad at me," he says, soft and concerned. I'm not sure if he's rubbing his eyes because he's tired or because he can't look at me. Either way, it's adorable. Everything he does is adorable.

I've gone from finding him completely annoying when I first knew him, to finding him moderately cute but still annoying, to finding everything he does perfectly cute. Except for the ignoring me part.

"I'm a little bit mad at you." I don't look at him.

"Well, a little bit is better than a lot."

"Okay, I'm a lot mad at you." I finally look at him, and he's still rubbing his eyes. I wonder again if he was up all night deciding whether he should come knock on Sunny's door. I wish I could read his mind. Just for a second. "You've been ignoring me for weeks. Since winter break."

"I haven't been ignoring you. I've just been, I don't know, busy. I guess."

"That's not a good excuse."

"I guess not," he says. As exciting as this conversation is, I want to go back to sleep. It feels like we're not getting anywhere. I could do this whole thing better if I was more awake. Maybe it's not a good idea to discuss important things in the middle of the night.

"Remember that day with the grapes?" I ask, after a few moments of quiet.

"Grapes?"

"We were at my house and we were throwing them into each other's mouth. It was warm for October."

"Oh. Yeah. I think so."

"That day felt perfect. Everything seemed like it was exactly the way it was supposed to be." I crinkle up my face, afraid that I may start to cry. That will only make me look worse than I'm sure I already do.

All Yamir says is, "I remember that day," and I know that we're not stale bread. Things can go back to being right again.

"Let's go back to that day."

"Luce-Juice, how many times do I have to tell you that I don't have a time machine?"

I laugh. Even in the middle of this awkward conversation at three in the morning, Yamir is still able to make me laugh. Then he starts laughing too, and soon we're just sitting on his couch completely cracking up.

This is why I like him so much. No one can make me laugh like Yamir makes me laugh.

I throw a pillow at his face. "You know what I mean," I say finally.

"I think I do."

We stare at each other for a few more seconds, and I pray that he doesn't try to kiss me. I'd need to brush my teeth or at least use mouthwash before a kiss. Thankfully, he grabs my hand and leads me back to the stairs.

"So, do you think you can stop ignoring me? Or what?" I ask.

"I think so," he says. "It seems easy enough."

"Um, okay." I can't tell what he means by that, but it seems like he understands what I'm saying and that he'll try to do better.

"Let's go back to sleep," he says.

I nod because my eyelids weigh a million pounds, and I don't think I have anything else to add. We walk upstairs and he drops me off at the door to Sunny's room.

I know I'll never fall back to sleep now. I replay the conversation over and over like a favorite song on repeat. I'm still not sure where we stand, but talking made me feel better.

He has to know that he can't ignore me—that things can't go on the way they were going.

Sometimes all it takes is talking to someone, hearing their voice, listening to what they say, to make everything seem better.

Lucy's tip for surviving eighth grade:
Talk to people you've never talked to before.

Mrs. Ramal makes her famous banana pancakes in the morning. She's using her restaurant-sized griddle. She always makes way more pancakes than we could ever eat, but something about that feels fun—an overflowing platter of pancakes in the middle of the table and maple syrup in a little glass pitcher. It's decadent.

Sunny and I get down to breakfast first. We're sipping fresh-squeezed grapefruit juice and looking through the stack of catalogs her mom keeps on the counter.

I have a sense of energy I haven't felt in a while. If my mood is this great after last night's conversation with Yamir, imagine how I would feel if things were actually perfect with us again.

I know in my brain that my life shouldn't revolve around Yamir. I should be able to be okay without him. I should be able to feel happy even if things aren't great between us.

Still, I'll enjoy the moment. I'll enjoy how I'm feeling right now.

A few minutes later Yamir comes down to breakfast. He's wearing mesh shorts and his Old Mill Middle School soccer shirt. It's torn and faded and looks like something a hip store would sell for a lot of money because it looks vintage.

"Yo," he says, not looking at anyone. He slumps down in the chair and pours himself a cup of juice. He starts reading Mrs. Ramal's Chadwicks catalog like it's the most interesting thing he's ever seen.

"Sleep well?" I ask, and he kicks me under the table.

"Yeah, like a baby." He looks up from the catalog and smirks. I love that smirk.

Mrs. Ramal brings over a sizzling platter of pancakes and we dig in. Well, I try to dig in. Normally I just eat and eat until I'm so stuffed it's hard to walk. But today is different. Today it's hard to eat around Yamir, and he notices.

"Luce-Juice, not hungry for the Ramal family favorite?"

"I've already had one pancake." It's kind of a lie because I've only had a few bites, but I doubt he's going to look at my plate that closely.

Sunny gives me a strange look and Yamir keeps eating.

"Well, I'm out of here. Basketball practice."

"How do you plan to get there?" Mrs. Ramal asks him.

"Clint's pops is driving us," he says, and just like that he's out of the kitchen. It's like our conversation last night never happened.

All at once I feel like the tires on my old bicycle. The day we got the bike they were sparkly, shiny, full of air. Now they're deflated and dusty in the corner of my garage. I shouldn't rest so much of my happiness on Yamir. If things are good, I feel great. And if they're bad, I feel horrid.

It's an unpredictable, broken, dangerous, seesaw way of living.

As we're finishing breakfast, Sunny's phone rings. It's Evan.

"Hold on a second. Let me ask Lucy," she says. "Evan wants to know if we want to go to the mall with him and those twins?"

"What twins?" I ask.

"You know, the new ones. Travis and Gavin or something?"

I think about my options. Do I want to go to the mall with them and probably have an okay time while thinking about Yamir most of the day? Or do I want to go home and spend all day thinking about Yamir and doing nothing?

My first option is way better. Plus, it's so nice that Sunny is including me. She's way better than she was last summer, when I felt left out.

"Sure. Sounds good."

Sunny gets back on the phone. "We're in. My mom will drop us off by Dreamer's Bar and Grill in, like, an hour."

"I'm the chauffeur, the chef, the butler, the maid," Mrs. Ramal says under her breath. "At least I know I'm needed around here." She laughs, so I know she's not mad.

"The pancakes were delicious as always," I tell her. "You can open up a bed-and-breakfast one day. I mean, when Sunny and Yamir are all grown up."

She smiles. "I'll consider it. Thanks, Lucy."

Sunny and I go upstairs to change—and I realize I have no clothes here. We came straight from the spa, and I didn't expect to go to the mall today.

"I need to borrow clothes again," I tell her.

"Take whatever you want." She's in the bathroom putting on eyeliner. She's not very good at it, so it takes her a while.

"Why are you being so nice to me?" I ask her when she gets out.

"Huh? What do you mean?"

I sit down on her bed. "I mean, you let me tag along with you and Evan, you lend me your clothes, you were quick on your feet suggesting that sleepover because you knew I didn't want to go to Scotty's with that group."

"My brother's a doofus. So I guess I feel partially responsible for all your suffering. Plus you're my best friend, and I love you." She throws a hooded sweatshirt at me. "Here, wear this. I know it's your favorite."

It's just a simple gray hoodie, but she's right—it is my favorite. Something about the way it's worn in and how it's not light gray but not dark gray either.

"Can I do your makeup before we go?"

Sunny glares at me. "Lucy. Hello. This is not last year. I don't need a confidence boost. I'm feeling pretty good these days."

"I know." I go to her bathroom and grab her makeup bag. "This is for me. I'm a ball of stress, and I think doing your makeup will calm me down."

Sunny rolls her eyes. "Fine. Anything for you. But not too much."

She sits in the swivel chair at her white vanity table and faces me. It only takes a few brushes of blush, and I'm calmer.

Things may be weird with Yamir, but at least I have Sunny. After all we've been through, Sunny is still by my side. Best friends are more important than boyfriends, anyway. Everyone needs a best friend, and I'm so glad she's mine.

Lucy's tip for surviving eighth grade:
Do your homework, but make time for fun too.

𝒲hen we get to the mall, Evan and the twins are already there.

"Hello, ladies," Evan says, like he's a fifty-year-old man. He's like a miniature dad, but I guess that's what Sunny likes about him. Even his long-sleeved polo looks like something my dad would wear.

We say hi, and Sunny and Evan do this shoulder-nudge thing they always do. It's kind of cute and less awkward than a kiss when others are around.

"Lucy, you know Travis and Gavin, right?"

I nod. "Do you guys ever go by Trav and Gav?"

They look at me a little oddly at first, but then they laugh.

"You guys are in band, right?" I ask them.

"Yup. He plays sax and I play clarinet," one of them says,

pointing to the other. They're identical, and I don't think I should even try to tell them apart. I'll never succeed.

"Cool. I play the flute."

"I've seen you around," one of them says, and I'm not sure what to make of that. I guess it's nice to be noticed even by someone you've never spoken to.

We wander around, and then the boys decide to go to the arcade.

"We'll wait for you out here," Sunny tells them. "We're not really into video games."

As soon as they're far enough away, Sunny turns to me. "Travis likes you," she says. "Evan just whispered that to me."

"Is he the one who plays the sax or the clarinet?"

Sunny bursts out laughing and I do too. I'm not sure why that was funny, but it was.

"You can't tell them apart?" Sunny asks.

"Nope. Can you?"

"Um, kind of, but only because Travis always wears plainer T-shirts and Gavin always wears something with a sports team on it."

"Okay. I'll try to keep that in mind." Soon we're both out of control cracking up, unable to stop. That always happens with Sunny and me. It starts with something just a little bit funny and then it turns into something completely hilarious.

The boys come out of the arcade because they ran out of money and find us sitting on the bench, laughing.

"What's so funny?" Gavin asks. I know it's him because he's the one wearing a Knicks T-shirt.

"They're always laughing," Evan explains. "Girls. You know how it is."

I look more closely at Travis as we walk. He's wearing a red hoodie. His hair is long in the front, and it's a mixture of red and brown. Could he be cute? I'm not sure. But it's funny how once you hear that someone likes you, they immediately seem cuter.

"So, where'd you guys move from?" I ask Travis when we're on our way to the food court. Gavin seems to only be interested in talking to Evan about sports, and I can tell that it's annoying Sunny. He just keeps going on and on about some game that happened in 1994. We weren't even born yet!

"Chicago," he says. "My dad got a new job."

"Oh, my sister goes to Northwestern," I tell him. "Do you miss it?"

He shrugs. "Kinda. I miss my friends."

"You'll make friends here," I tell him. "Just give it a little while."

"I know. I just need time to adjust, I think."

Wow. I never knew boys thought about this kind of stuff. Travis seems unusually nice.

"Have you lived here your whole life?" he asks me.

"Yup. I think it's the best town in the world. You'll like it. Just wait until summer—that's when it's really the best."

"Really?" he asks, and we make eye contact. His eyes are green with little brown specks. It almost looks like someone painted them that way.

"Yeah. Definitely. And it's hard to tell how great a place is in the winter. I mean, I know you moved in September, but still. You need to see Old Mill in the summer to really appreciate it."

"Okay, I can't wait."

We get in line at Hotdogger & Co., and Evan starts to tell Travis and Gavin all about the hot-dog-eating contest last summer.

"It was crazy," he says. "You would not believe how many hot dogs Lucy ate."

"How many?" Travis asks me.

"Like, fifteen, maybe?" I say, half-embarrassed, half-proud.

He high-fives me. "That's insanely awesome."

This Travis kid is growing on me. And even though it's only been a few hours, I can totally tell the twins apart now.

We stay at the mall until five in the afternoon, and then Sunny's mom calls and says she has to pick us up because they have dinner plans.

"We gotta go," Sunny tells the boys. "My parents are going out tonight, so this is our only ride."

"Oh, party at Sunny's house!" Gavin says. I'm getting the feeling that he may be the wilder one of the two.

"Nah, not tonight." Sunny smiles. "I'll keep it in mind for another night, though."

I can't imagine Sunny throwing a party. Maybe Yamir. But Sunny, no.

We're waiting for Sunny's mom to pick us up, and the boys are waiting for Evan's mom. This weekend was not at all what I expected when school ended on Friday. I don't know what I expected exactly, but it wasn't this. Erica and Zoe at the spa, an impromptu sleepover at Sunny's, a middle-of-the-night talk with Yamir, and then a mall day with a new boy who may have a crush on me.

I know I'm going to have trouble falling asleep again tonight.

Be polite even when you don't feel like it.

Mrs. Deleccio finds me as soon as I get to school Monday morning.

"Lucy, the school board tells me they'll have a final decision this afternoon. They'd like all of you to meet with them at 3:45 in the school library. Can you do that?"

I run over my schedule in my head; I don't have anything going on. "Sure. I think so."

"Okay, great. I'll try to tell the others, but if you see them before I do, please let them know."

"Okay, thanks."

She caught me off guard, and I had to think for a minute to figure out what decision she was talking about. But of course this is the big moment for our green cafeteria plan! Now I have to get through the rest of the day wondering what the decision is going to be.

If it was bad news, they probably wouldn't want to meet with us. They'd just e-mail or something. But if it was good news, would they really need a meeting? They could just say that everything looks perfect, and we could move on from there.

I have no idea what the decision will be.

And I won't see Sunny until third period. Today is a gym day, so our regular schedule is different. We're not in the same gym class. And I have band and she has orchestra.

I walk into the band room, and Travis is the first person I see.

I had fun with him Saturday, but Sunny's comment about his crush on me is irking me a bit. I mean, I don't even know if it's true. But if it is true, I don't know what to do about it. I still like Yamir. He drives me totally crazy, but he's Yamir. He's in a class of his own. I can't abandon all hope that things will work out between us.

"Hi, Lucy," Travis says.

"Hey." At the mall he seemed cuter and I felt chattier. But now, in the band room on a Monday morning, I wish he wouldn't talk at all. Maybe it's the fluorescent lighting, or the fact that my stomach is already grumbling because I'm hungry for lunch. But I just had a snack on the way to class, so it can't be hunger.

My grumbling stomach must be from nervousness. Talking to Travis is making me nervous. This can't be good.

"Your mall is cool," he says, and I nod, and then he goes over to his seat in the clarinet section.

I was rude. I know I was. But sometimes it's too early to talk to someone you don't know that well. Making conversation takes energy. And I'm not a morning person.

Mr. Flagg stands up in front of the band and tells us that we need to take things more seriously. "Take time with your instruments. Don't just throw them in your locker or under a pile of laundry," he says. "Take time to get to know them. Don't consider practicing a chore."

I look over at Travis as Mr. Flagg is talking. The rest of the band is mumbling to each other and not paying attention, but Travis actually seems to care.

I shouldn't have dismissed him a few minutes ago. He seems to be different from all the other boys at school.

When I get to lunch, everyone's already at the table. Annabelle is picking at her wrap, and Georgina has a steaming plate of cafeteria pasta in front of her. Sunny's eating an Indian dish that her mom must have made for dinner the night before.

"Hey," I mumble, still tired.

"We have the perfect plan for you," Eve says, picking all the onions out of her salad. "We heard what happened."

I start to think back over the weekend, but I'm not sure what she's talking about. Then I realize—Travis. They've heard he likes me, and they probably think I'm the worst person ever.

"If you and Yamir ever want to hang out alone, you can just go to the spa after hours!" Eve makes this declaration like it's the answer to all the world's problems, like she just came up with the solution for peace in the Middle East.

"Oh, um, right." I smile and unwrap my sandwich.

"You have a key, right?" Eve asks.

I nod. "I do. Good idea. Thanks, Eve."

It's clear she's trying to help me. I guess she's worried that Yamir and I don't have enough alone time. And since Eve is so obsessed with boyfriends and high school and basically anything grown-up, I get why she's all revved up about this.

"What do you think he's going to get you for Valentine's Day?" Annabelle asks, getting a tiny dot of mayonnaise in the corner of her mouth.

"Valentine's Day? Isn't that, like, pretty far away?" I ask. It feels like Christmas and Hanukkah were yesterday.

Georgina twirls some pasta around her fork, but it's hard to do with a cheap plastic one. It'll be better when we have the reusable metal forks. *If* we have them, I should say. If the school board says yes tonight. "Lucy, it's the second week of January," Georgina says. "It's going to be here before you know it. And it's a really big deal when you have a boyfriend. You can't forget about it."

"Thanks, Georgina. I won't." I look at Sunny and hope she can read my eyes. What has gotten into these girls? It seems like all they want to do is give me relationship advice.

"We're just jealous," Annabelle admits. "I know that most people hide their jealousy, but we don't."

"Be jealous of Sunny!" I say, louder than I'd planned. "She has a boyfriend too, you know."

"Lucy!" Sunny says. "You just yelled, and now Mr. Davenport is coming over."

"What's the trouble, girls?" He asks. The ink from his pen has seeped through the pocket of his button-down shirt. He's like the nerdy teacher on every TV show ever made.

"Nothing. Sorry for yelling, Mr. D." I smile at him. "We'll be quieter."

"Thank you, Lucy." He stays for a minute or two just to make sure everything's actually fine, I guess. And then he walks away.

"Sorry I yelled," I whisper. "I guess all I'm saying is that it's cool to have a boyfriend and stuff. But you'll have boyfriends soon enough, and it's weird when people are jealous of you. Plus, it's not like having a boyfriend is the be-all and end-all of the world." I heard my mom use that expression once, but I'm not totally sure what it means.

They look at me suspiciously, so I decide to drop the topic. Sunny pats my leg under the table. It's good that she's on my side, or at least knows what's going on. But I wonder how long she's going to let me keep up the charade that Yamir and I are a model couple.

When I decided I needed to have the most perfect end to middle school, this was definitely not what I had in mind. But when I made that decision, I didn't know that Yamir would disappear on me.

"We also heard about Travis," Eve adds, clearly not interested in talking about anything other than boys. "The whole thing kind of reminds me of this book I read a few months ago—the girl had to choose between two cute boys, and it was so tragic. But anyway, I guess Travis doesn't know that you're going out with the cutest boy in Old Mill."

"Eve!" Sunny's the one yelling now. "Stop! My brother. Gross."

Eve makes eyes at me. "It's true," she mouths.

I'll never be able to tell Eve the truth. That things aren't so great with Yamir and me. That there barely even is a Yamir and me.

It would be like when your favorite actors break up, or in her case, two characters in a great romance novel. It would break her heart. Maybe as much as it would break mine.

Lucy's tip for surviving eighth grade:
Take deep breaths when you're overwhelmed.

Sunny waits for me after studio art, my last-period class. Sunny's taking ceramics instead, so we always wait for each other in the art wing on art day.

"Ready for the meeting?" she asks.

"Nervous," is all I can manage to say.

We walk to the library together, and the closer we get, the more nervous I am. All these adults on the school board left work early for this meeting. I guess they think it's really important.

Mrs. Deleccio is already there with Clint's dad and the other members of the school board. It looks like Mrs. Casale, the new librarian, has broken her "no eating in the library" rule, because there's a plate of cookies on the table and a pitcher of cucumber-flavored water.

"This seems fancy, doesn't it?" Sunny whispers to me.

"Yeah, Mrs. Deleccio usually buys the generic brand, but those look like they're from One Girl Cookies, down by the water. It's almost too fancy."

"I know." Sunny clenches my hand. "Now I'm nervous."

"Welcome, girls. Come have a seat." Mrs. Deleccio smiles, and I take that to mean good news is coming. I'm the kind of person who always reads into things, even when I probably shouldn't. I convince myself of signs when they're probably just coincidences.

Evan and Annabelle arrive a few minutes later. We all find seats around the library table.

"Dig in, please," Mrs. Deleccio insists, passing the plate of cookies around.

"We're thrilled with all the work you've done," Clint's dad starts. "We all met and discussed it, and then we realized something."

Oh God. Did they realize that it costs too much to make the cafeteria green? That they actually don't care about the environment? That we missed something huge in our report?

My heart is thumping in my chest, louder than when Russell Chapman plays the bass drum in band.

"We realized it's not enough to make only the Old Mill Middle School cafeteria green. We need to make *all* the schools green—the elementary school and the high school too. The faculty rooms, the catered events, the conferences." He picks up a cookie from the plate and takes a bite. "Delicious," he says to Mrs. Deleccio.

"Oh, I didn't bake them." She gets nervous all of a sudden, and I want Clint's dad to go back to discussing the stuff about going green. Who cares about the cookies?

"It's a huge undertaking," he continues. "But we can do it. It will end up being more cost-effective too, if we're ordering for a whole district. And we don't want your work to end here. You'll all be at the high school in the fall, and we're going to need lots more help."

"I'm in!" Annabelle says in her enthusiastic, kiss-up Annabelle voice. But right now, I don't even mind. I feel the same way.

"Me too," I tell everyone. "Thanks so much for being excited about this, and for taking us seriously."

"Taking you seriously? Of course! You're making a huge difference," Clint's dad says.

"Thanks," I reply.

Annabelle starts, "And Lucy knows a lot about the high school because—"

I cut her off. "Because my sister Claudia went there!" Annabelle raises her eyebrows at me like she's shocked. But I know where she was going with that, and I don't see any reason why Clint's dad needs to know about Yamir and me. Clint and Yamir are best friends, so maybe Clint's dad already knows. Or maybe he doesn't know anything. Either way, we don't need to bring it up. "So, what are the next steps?"

"E-mail your list of vendors to me." He hands me his card, and I feel so official. I'm not sure anyone has ever given me a business card before. "As soon as the vendors can get everything in order, we'll transform the cafeterias!"

Mrs. Deleccio jumps in next. "Mr. Titone, the head of cafeteria services for the district, will be taking this over, for the most part. He already knows this is in the works, and I'm sure he'll hear from his boss, but it would be nice if someone from Earth Club also fills him in."

"I can do that," Evan says. "He lives around the corner from me. I used to play baseball with his son."

"That sounds great, Evan."

It seems like our work is mostly done—at least until we get to be in the high school Earth Club. I can't tell if I'm happy or sad. Maybe a little of both.

This must be how runners feel after a marathon—so happy to have completed it, but unsure what to do next.

How will I spend my time? What will I work on? I think I need to come up with another Earth Club project, or my life will seem really incomplete.

We chat for a little while longer about average Old Mill stuff—the traveling soccer team and the community pool that's being remodeled for next summer. I love to talk about improvements in Old Mill, but right now I can't focus. I'm too excited that this cafeteria thing is really happening, and too sad that my work on it is mostly done.

I want to go home and talk to Mom, Dad, and Grandma. I want to call Claudia.

Most of all, I want to talk to Yamir.

Lucy's tip for surviving eighth grade:
Celebrate all the good things, no matter how small.

 $\mathcal{A}$nnabelle's mom offers to drive Sunny and me home, and I'm immediately disappointed. I was a little bit excited for the chance that Sunny's mom would pick us up and Yamir would be in the car. But there's no good reason for us to say no.

Mom and Grandma are sitting in the living room drinking tea when I get home.

"Who's Travis?" Mom asks before she even says hi.

"Huh?"

"A boy named Travis stopped by the pharmacy today," Grandma explains. "He looked lost, wandering around for a little too long. So I asked him if he needed help, and then he asked if someone named Lucy worked there."

"Oh. Yeah, he's new. We go to school together."

"Got it." Mom smiles like she thinks something is up,

even though nothing really is. She gets these ideas in her head and blows them totally out of proportion.

"Anyway, I have good news." I sit down next to Mom and grab her mug for a sip of tea.

"Yeah?" Grandma asks, impatient as usual.

"The school board proposal went through," I tell them. "Our cafeteria will be green! And not just ours. The elementary school and the high school too!"

"Really?" Mom jumps up. "Tell us more! Tell us more!"

"Okay, calm down." I laugh at Mom's enthusiasm, then explain all about Clint's dad and how it's going to work. I have to stop every few seconds because Mom has so many questions, but it doesn't bother me. When you're really excited about something, you don't mind when people ask questions about it. You want to tell them everything so that they can be excited too.

"That is so wonderful, darling," Grandma says. "I can't even believe it. My granddaughter is taking over the world!"

"Well, if that's the case, the least you can do is treat me to a celebratory dinner." I give them a hopeful look. "Sushi, anyone?"

Grandma and Mom glance at each other. I think their eyes are saying yes.

"Sure! Go call Dad and let him know," Mom says. "He

was expecting baked ziti leftovers, but something tells me he'll be okay with this."

"It's settled. Sushi it is. We'll leave at 6:45." Grandma collects the mugs and goes into the kitchen.

"Do you want to invite Yamir?" Mom whispers with a sneaky expression on her face.

"Why are you whispering and what is that face?" I ask. All my happy feelings wash away, and I'm suddenly annoyed.

"I didn't want Grandma to yell at me for butting into your business." Mom is still whispering.

"Oh." I think for a second. "It'll be better if it's just us tonight. But thanks."

They were so excited for me that I didn't want to tell them how I'm also feeling a little sad and uncertain about Yamir. I want them to think I'm taking over the world, not stressing about a boy. I guess I can just focus on being happy for now and worry about the empty feeling later.

I go up to my room to check my e-mail, change clothes, and get ready for dinner. Going out for sushi with my family isn't like going out for any other meal. We take it really seriously. We order one huge round to start. And we order as much as we want after that. We eat and eat and eat until we're so stuffed it's hard for us to walk out to the car.

It's a very special treat.

We're all big sushi eaters, even Grandma. She says that she's going to take everyone to Japan when she wins the lottery. The weird thing is that she hardly ever plays the lottery, so I'm not sure how that's going to happen. Still, it's fun to think about.

I sign in to check my e-mail, but there's nothing exciting there: a message from Bloomingdale's about a sale, and some mass e-mail about Eighth-Grade Masquerade that I don't feel like reading.

So I draft an e-mail to Claudia and Bean:

Guess what? The cafeteria is officially going green! And not just the middle school—the high school and elementary school too! Yippee! Hope all is well in Chicago! A new kid in school just moved from there. He said his mom misses it a lot.
Smooches, Lucy

I click SEND and then draft an e-mail to Yamir:

Well, I rocked the cafeteria thing! Going green in a major way. Call/text/whatever and I will fill you in. Sushi tonight. I know you're jealous. xo

I hit SEND before I can change my mind about the "xo." It was probably a mistake. Maybe we're not at the "xo" point anymore. Who knows where we are now. Probably "sincerely" or "talk soon."

I decide to write a quick e-mail to Mrs. Deleccio too. I don't want my work with Earth Club to be over, and I think there's one more project I can take on before I graduate: composting. It's something people are talking about a lot these days. Some towns are even instituting mandatory composting programs. It seems like the logical next step for us.

Hi Mrs. Deleccio,
I had an idea I wanted to run by you. Now that the cafeteria will be green, we need to focus on our food waste! What if we started a composting program? I'd love to take this on. Let me know what you think.
Thanks, Lucy

I love that we can e-mail teachers. It makes everything so much easier. And it means I might not have to wait until next Monday's meeting to hear what she thinks of my idea.

Dad texts me to say that he'll pick us up and drive us to the sushi place, since he's already out running errands and will be passing the house anyway. This may be true, but I think he just wants to show off his new car. He got some revamped old convertible, and he'll probably ask if we want the top down even though it's freezing outside. It's silly now, but it's going to be awesome when the weather warms up.

I text Sunny that we're going out for sushi, because she loves it almost as much as I do, and I'm secretly hoping she'll say something about Yamir, mention where he is or that he's heard about the cafeteria.

But she doesn't write back. That is so unlike her. I wonder if she lost her phone.

I finish getting ready and go downstairs to wait for Dad. He picks us up exactly on time. Mom sits in front and Grandma and I sit in the backseat. It's a rare four-door convertible, bright red with beige leather seats. I wonder if Dad will let Claudia drive it when she's home on break. We can drive around together and go to the movies in style! I hope he still has this car when I get my license in three years. Maybe he'll be bored of it by then and let me drive it all the time.

Dad drops us off in front of Sushi of Gari, because the parking lot is full and he needs to look for street parking. This isn't unusual. It's the most popular sushi place in all of Connecticut. People drive for hours to eat here.

I see two things as soon as I walk in. And even though the

sushi here is the most delicious in the world, I immediately want to run out and go home.

Travis and his family are sitting in the booth by the side window.

And the Ramals are sitting at the round table in the back.

My stomach hurts so much that I don't think I'll be able to eat a single piece of sushi tonight. In fact, I may never be able to eat again.

14

𝒯𝒽𝒶𝓃𝓀𝒻𝓊𝓁𝓁𝓎, 𝓃ℴ ℴ𝓃ℯ ℯ𝓁𝓈ℯ in my family sees the Ramals, and they don't really know Travis so they don't notice that he's there. I text Sunny:

Meet me in the bathroom. I'm at Gari too.

I wait and wait and wait, but again, no text back. She must have left her phone at home. It's the only explanation, since she never turns it off.

The hostess seats us at a table by the window on the other side of the restaurant. My back is to Travis, but out of the corner of my eye I can kind of see Yamir. I think they're approaching the end of their meal, since most of their plates are empty except for a few stray pieces of ginger and uneven clumps of wasabi.

"Well, this is exciting," Dad says. "Sushi with my favorite ladies!"

"Oh, Sam," Grandma says. "Such a charmer." I'm not sure if she's teasing Dad or not. Even though I've known Grandma all my life, I can never tell exactly what she's thinking.

Kai, our favorite waiter, comes over to take our order, even though he knows exactly what we like: pretty much one of everything and extra-spicy tuna rolls. Soon he brings over our edamame and glasses of water with lime, and I start to relax.

No one knows I'm here. Maybe it's better that Sunny forgot her phone and that she doesn't know I'm here. And they probably won't have to walk by us as they leave. This is a pay-your-waiter kind of place, and we're not sitting by the door.

I'm safe. I can eat and enjoy my sushi without having to see Yamir or Travis.

But ten minutes pass and the Ramals are still sitting there. What are they waiting for?

I want to go to the bathroom so I can sneak a glance and see if they've paid their check, but that seems like a bad idea because then they'll see me.

"Luce, you okay?" Mom asks. "This is a celebration for you, and you seem like you're about to be arrested."

"Jane!" Grandma yelps. "What kind of thing is that to say to your daughter?"

Mom rolls her eyes. "Ma. I'm not saying she's going to be arrested. I'm saying that's how she's acting."

"Oh Lord," Grandma says under her breath. The last thing I need right now is for them to get into a fight. So I put on a smile and continue eating edamame. I just need to pretend that no one I know is here.

We finish the edamame, and Dad's miso soup comes— and then it seems like all the craziness that could possibly happen happens all at once.

Kai brings over a platter of sushi pieces, everything we like: tuna, salmon, yellowtail, fatty tuna, and a bunch of other stuff that I always forget the names of. He's adjusting it on the table when Mom knocks over a cup of water.

Grandma holds her head in frustration. She acts like Mom just lit the restaurant on fire.

"No big deal. No big deal," Dad says in his calm, "everything's okay" voice. To be fair, this is pretty much his everyday voice.

Kai sends a busboy over to clean it, and then I'm not sure how this happens exactly, but it seems like Mom elbows him accidentally. The busboy stumbles and falls. The owner of the restaurant, Gari himself, comes over to see what's going on.

And that's when the Ramals decide to leave.

"Everything okay here, Desbergs?" Mr. Ramal asks, laughing.

"You are all going to be kicked out and asked to never return."

I'm glad he thinks this is so funny.

"Everything's fine." I smile but don't turn around. I can't tell if Yamir is there with his dad or not. I'm praying that he walked out the other way.

Someone taps my shoulder, and I'm scared to turn around until I hear, "Funny seeing you here," in her classic Sunny giggly voice.

"Well, you would have known if you'd checked your phone!" I say, sounding too angry for someone eating at Sushi of Gari. I finally turn around.

Sunny is standing there with both Yamir and Travis.

Forget about eating all the delicious sushi that's on the table. All I care about right now is not getting sick in front of everyone at this restaurant.

My parents are talking to Sunny's parents, and of course I'm trying to eavesdrop. It might be my imagination, but I swear that Mrs. Ramal says, "Yamir insisted we eat here tonight. We never go to restaurants during the week."

Did I just make that up? No. She really said it.

Maybe he wanted to eat here because he knows it's my favorite restaurant. If you think Sushi of Gari, you automatically think Lucy Desberg. He was thinking about me. I'll take it. It's a step in the right direction.

Or did he see my e-mail? And assume we'd come here to celebrate? That's a possibility too.

"So, what's new, Yamir?" I ask, trying to play it cool.

"Nada." He looks at his phone, seemingly bored.

Fine. I guess that's how he's going to be.

Travis is still standing there. He hasn't said anything. Shouldn't he be eating with his family?

I look over to their table and see Gavin and their parents eating away. Travis is going to miss out on all the good sushi.

I say, "Travis, I see you've discovered the best restaurant in all of Connecticut."

"Of course! My dad eats at the sushi places in Manhattan whenever he has a meeting."

"Smart man."

"So, I heard all about the cafeteria decision." He raises a hand for a high-five. "Way to go, Lucy. That's awesome."

I look over at Yamir, who is still standing there, leaning on my grandma's chair and staring at his phone. He should just go wait at the front of the restaurant if he's so bored here.

"Thanks so much, Travis. But, um, you should go eat. You're gonna miss out on all the sushi." I nudge my head in the direction of his family's table.

"Uh. Yeah. You're right." He gives an embarrassed smile. "See you in school."

He walks away, and Yamir finally looks up. "That kid is *weeeeiiiirrrrdddd.*"

"No, he isn't." Sunny hits him on the arm. "He's nice and cool, not a complete doofus like you and your friends."

He hits Sunny back. "Right. Okay. Because you really know about being cool."

"Okay, children, time to go," Mrs. Ramal says. "The Desbergs need to enjoy their dinner."

"Bye, Luce," Sunny says. "I'll text you."

Yamir says nothing but does this strange hand-gesture thing where he puts two fingers on his forehead and then points them at me. I've never seen it before, and I have no idea what it means.

"Everything okay here?" Gari comes by again, putting a hand on Dad's shoulder. It's a little unusual, because he knows Dad the least well of all of us, but yet he seems to feel this connection to him. Maybe it's a guy thing.

"Wonderful as always," Grandma says. She does this funny thing with sushi where she moves her chopsticks all around while she decides what piece to pick. I've never told her that I notice this, because I'm afraid she'll stop doing it. It's just so cute.

"Now we can enjoy our dinner," Mom says. "No more interruptions. Who's ready for round two?"

The platters are mostly empty, and I'm not even sure I've had any sushi yet.

"I am," I say. Now that the Ramals are gone and I've convinced Travis to stay at his table, I can eat in peace.

We order a second round, and we're eating more than chatting, which is fine with me, since it means they're not asking about Yamir and Travis. I'm sure my family has a million questions. Well, at least my mom does. I can see it on her face.

"Lucy, we're so proud of you and all the work you've done with Earth Club," Dad says eventually. "You put your all into it and it paid off."

"Thanks." I smile. I'm so appreciative of this, but all I can think about is what just happened with Yamir and Travis.

We order three rounds of sushi, and by the time we're done, we're fuller than we've ever been before.

"Thanks so much for coming," Gari says. "See you soon, I hope."

"We might not need to eat again for three weeks," Dad mumbles. "So full. *So* so full."

"That's how we like it." Gari pats him on the back, and we walk out to the car.

That may have been the strangest sushi-eating experience of my life. And that includes one time when I'm pretty sure my dad ate a live fish.

15

Lucy's tip for surviving eighth grade:
Have faith that things will eventually work out.

My good feelings about Yamir coming to Sushi of Gari—proof that he was thinking about me—pretty much evaporated after he didn't say good-bye. And he still hasn't replied to my e-mail.

Eighth grade keeps getting stranger and stranger. It feels like the time we took the high-speed ferry to Block Island for vacation. The boat wobbled and swayed so much before it even started out.

Right now I'm in the wobbly phase, and I have a feeling that most of what's going to happen hasn't even started yet.

I'm not sure why I was so confident that I could make this the best semester yet. I was so sure of it, and it didn't seem that hard to accomplish. But with each day that passes, I seem to get further and further away from the possibility of perfection.

Take right now, for example. Erica Crane and Zoe Feldman are sitting at our lunch table. Not just stopping by, or kicking a chair as they pass, or knocking over a milk container.

They're actually sitting here, eating their lunches.

Erica has some kind of fancy mozzarella and tomato salad from Antonio's Italian Deli downtown. And Zoe's eating a bagel with cream cheese.

"So, I heard a rumor about you, Lucy, and I think I might need you to help me," Zoe says between bites.

"Yeah?" I ask. Zoe doesn't make me as nervous as Erica does, but she still makes me a little nervous. I'm scared she'll ask me something really personal in front of everyone at the table, like how many boys I've kissed or something. I don't completely trust her.

"So, everyone is talking about how Travis likes you," she starts.

"They are?" I exclaim. That can't be good. I mean, it's flattering and everything. But technically I still have a boyfriend. A boyfriend who I really like—even though he's a total jerk.

Erica gives me a look that seems to say I've been living on another planet.

"Yeah. I mean, everyone knows," Zoe says.

"Oh. Um. Okay."

"Wait until Yami-pajami finds out," Erica sings, like she's happy about this news.

I ignore her. "So, what do you need my help with?" I ask Zoe.

"I like Gavin." Zoe sounds confident and proud of herself somehow. "I want to go to the Masquerade with him."

"I don't really know Gavin," I say.

"Right. But we'll get to know him. Together." Zoe wipes the cream cheese off her hands and puts an arm around me. "And then can you teach me that amazing eyeliner trick that Erica's told me about."

I nod. I don't understand what is happening here. Zoe needing my help. A boy telling the whole class he likes me.

"I think I have an idea for you," I tell Zoe. "Come with me after lunch, and I'll explain."

People always tell me that I worry about grown-up problems: saving the pharmacy, getting the grant, helping the eco-spa get off the ground. And that's true—I do worry about grown-up problems, and I find a way to solve them.

But now I have real thirteen-year-old problems to worry about. And I have no idea how to handle any of them.

I get home from school and find two e-mails from Clint's dad. I don't know if it's funny or pathetic, but I get more e-mails from him than I do from boys my own age.

He's reminding me to send him the list of the vendors we

researched, so he can make sure they're all approved by the food services director. Easy enough.

I look through the rest of my e-mails and realize that Claudia hasn't written me back. Neither has Bean. That's so unlike them. Maybe they're busy. But with what? First-semester finals are over.

I want to ask Mom, Dad, or Grandma if they've heard from Claudia or Bean, but if they haven't they'll start to worry, and I don't ever want to be the person who causes others to worry. As a worrier myself, I know the feeling quite well. And it's not fun!

Sunny calls me a few minutes later to tell me a Zoe story. "You're not going to believe what happened in social studies."

"What?"

"We had to act out a moment in history. But we could do whatever we wanted—a skit or a song or whatever. You know what I mean?"

"Yeah."

"So, that kid Gavin gets up to do a rap about the Civil War—and then Zoe just runs up and joins in! She didn't know the words at all; she just made stuff up, and did weird arm movements and stuff."

"Like, in front of the class?" I ask. My heart starts pounding. Maybe my way of helping Zoe with Gavin wasn't so helpful. Maybe it was a disaster. Suddenly I'm regretting everything.

I stop my Claudia stalking so I can pay attention to what Sunny is saying. But I'll have to get back to that soon. Claudia hasn't been on any of her social media sites lately, and she hasn't updated her blog. It's starting to really worry me.

She's missing.

"Hello? Are you hearing me?"

"Yes, yes, she did weird arm movements and joined the rap!" I need her to get to the end of this story. I'm scared that I'm responsible for something really terrible.

"And then she hugged Gavin in front of the class when it finished!" Sunny yelps. "How ridiculous is that?"

"Pretty ridiculous, but also pretty cool." I sigh with relief. Hugging seems okay. Not too crazy. She didn't say Gavin ran away screaming or anything. "I guess she doesn't need my help anymore."

Sunny laughs. "Well, the bad news is I don't think he likes her."

"Really?" My heart sinks like a brick in a swimming pool. I don't know Zoe that well, but I want her to be happy and get what she wants. "What makes you say that?"

"Just a hunch."

I can't tell Sunny that I actually gave Zoe the idea about

joining the rap. At the mall, I overheard Gavin talking about it, and I figured it would be a perfect way for Zoe to interact with him. At least, I thought it was a good idea at first. But now I'm not so sure.

I did try to help her, though. That should count for something.

My phone alerts me that I have a new e-mail so I get excited, but it's just a notice about a sale at the yoga store near the pharmacy.

Sunny and I are quiet on the phone for a moment, which isn't unusual for us, but then I hear something in the background.

Laughter. Girl laughter.

"Who's at your house?" I ask, assuming that Annabelle came to do homework, though it would have been weird if Sunny didn't invite me.

"You don't want to know," Sunny says.

"Huh?"

"That girl Sienna is here. Allegedly working on a science project with my brother."

I remember that feeling I had at sushi the other night, when my heart was hopping out of my body, but I realize that right now I am experiencing the exact opposite feeling: my heart is shriveling into a tiny raisin, dropping to the floor, and landing beside my feet.

"Oh," is all I can manage to say.

"She's one of those giggly girls." Sunny pauses. "It's driving me crazy."

"Sun, I have to go. Talk to you later." I hang up when the tears start pooling in the corners of my eyes and trickling down my cheeks.

If Yamir invited Sienna to his house to hang out, two things are very, very clear: first of all, Yamir and I are over. And I don't even know when it happened. Or why it happened. Or if there's anything I could have done about it.

Second of all: my whole plan for a perfect last semester is over too. Disappeared. Evaporated. Hopeless. Yamir doesn't like me anymore. I'm also failing at helping Zoe.

I'm pretty sure I'm on a path to have the worst semester ever.

16

Lucy's tip for surviving eighth grade:
Make sure to get fresh air, even when it's freezing.

"Lucy?" I hear someone calling me from far off in the distance. I assume the person is talking to another Lucy, because it's six o'clock in the evening in the middle of January and I'm sitting on one of the boardwalk benches, all alone.

I bet they're calling to Lucy their dog. Lucy is a surprisingly popular name for a dog.

But then I hear it again. And the voice is getting closer.

"Lucy," Evan says. "What are you doing here?"

I turn around to face him. "What are *you* doing here?"

"We run on the beach for cross-country," he says.

I should have guessed cross-country. He's in his Old Mill Middle School red sweat suit.

"Right."

"So now you have to tell me why you're here, because I know you're not on cross-country."

"Ha! I can't run at all." I smile. It feels like the first time I've laughed in a really long time.

"So spill it. I don't have forever. Coach Tello is going to be ready to go soon."

He sits down next to me on the bench and takes off his hat. His hair is sweaty, even though it's freezing.

"I needed a quiet place to think," I tell him. "And I hate Yamir."

"You do not hate Yamir," he says.

"No, really. I know I've said it before. But this time it's true."

He looks at me. "What happened?"

Evan and Yamir were friends when we were all in middle school, but I don't think they talk much anymore. Yamir moved on to high school and thinks he's too cool for everyone.

It's been a few days since Sienna was at his house, but everything feels fresh in my mind, like it happened five minutes ago. I tell Evan the whole story, and I don't leave out any details. I tell him about the sleepover, and our talk, and Sushi of Gari, and how Sienna was at his house.

"I know that girl," he says. "She just moved here, right? She lives around the corner from me."

"I hate her too."

"Lucy Desberg! I have never heard you talk this way in all the years I've known you." He's trying to make me laugh again, but so far it's not working.

When I don't say anything, Evan says, "Listen, just ignore him. Don't text or call him or anything. Act like you don't care at all."

"I've tried that. But there's one problem."

"What?"

"I do care. I care a lot."

"Evan! Come on! The bus is leaving." We hear Coach Tello calling from the entrance to the boardwalk.

"If you ever want to talk to someone that's not Sunny or the other girls at your table, I'm here." He gives me a soft tap on the shoulder and runs off toward the bus.

Evan just may be the person to talk to.

I can't really talk to Sunny, because Yamir is her brother. And Annabelle and the rest of the lunch girls think I have this blissful life with an amazing boyfriend and another boy who likes me. I mean, that's kind of what I want them to think, but it's not true at all. I can't burst their bubble. And how would I explain the whole thing? I'd have to admit I've pretty much been lying the whole time.

* * *

I spend the next week really working on not caring. It's probably going to take some practice, but I'm positive I can do it. When I put my mind to something, I know I can make it happen. Plus, it's a little easier not to care when there's another boy paying so much attention to you.

Travis. It turns out he is a pretty determined person too. And he's determined to get me to like him.

"Come over Saturday night," he says as we're on our way to band.

"Just me?" I ask. I've been talking to Travis more and more in band, telling myself I'm gathering Gavin information for Zoe. It's helpful to have something to focus on. I haven't really done much yet on my new Earth Club project, but in the meantime, playing matchmaker is good. And it's always more fun to help someone else. I'm hoping he'll tell me that Zoe should come over too.

"Well, no. Gavin and I are having a party."

"Is it your birthday?" I ask. Claudia went to parties all the time in high school, and they always made Grandma so nervous. Usually the parents were away and they ended really late and Claudia came home crying. I hope Travis is talking about a different kind of party.

"No. We used to have parties all the time in Chicago. So we wanted to try one out here." He smiles. "Nothing crazy.

Just pizza and soda, and we can hang out in our basement."

"Oh. Um, okay."

He smiles at me. "Don't sound so unsure. It's a finished basement, and we have a pool table and foosball and an old-fashioned pinball machine. It'll be chill."

"The pinball machine really makes it for me," I tease. "Now I'll definitely come."

He hits my arm gently. "Okay. Great."

He walks into band before me, and it's amazing what you can notice about a person when they're a few steps ahead of you: his jeans are a little too short and his sweatshirt is a little too long, but he has a cute walk. A confident walk. There's something nerdy about Travis. A cool kind of nerdy; he's not really trying to be anything other than who he is.

Georgina is the first one at our lunch table, and when I sit down she says, "I heard you were invited to the party."

"Hello to you too!" I laugh, but she doesn't.

"Are we all invited?" she asks.

"I think so." I open my lunch bag to find a peanut butter and jelly sandwich, and I immediately feel disappointed. Maybe I should start making my own lunches. "I mean, if you're not, I'll just make sure you are. Travis isn't the kind of person to leave people out."

"Cool." Georgina looks relieved. "Thanks, Lucy."

Everyone else comes late to lunch, so for a while it's just Georgina and me sitting there. And that's when it occurs to me—my new mission in life, now that the cafeteria project has succeeded.

Maybe I can't control everything to have the perfect last semester. But there's one thing I can do. And part of it is sitting right in front of me.

Annabelle, Georgina, and Eve are so concerned about having boyfriends. I've known the AGE girls, as these inseparable friends call themselves, forever—it's time for them to be happy. We only have a few more months of eighth grade, and I want those months to be awesome for them. I may not know Zoe that well, but I also want things to work out for her and Gavin.

I may not be able to control my own love life, but I can help all of them. And when you help other people, you feel better. It's a fact of life.

Lucy's tip for surviving eighth grade:
Remember that every one of your favorite experiences
was a new experience once.

"What are you wearing to the party?" Sunny asks me over the phone on Saturday. I've been online most of the day researching composting programs in schools. It's actually much more work than I realized. And I bet everyone is going to find it really gross. It'll definitely be harder to convince people to compost than it was to turn the cafeteria green. "This is kind of a big deal. It's like our first *party* party."

"We've been to thousands of birthday parties."

"Yeah, but this is, like, different. Boys are throwing a party just for the sake of a party."

"I guess so, yeah." For the first time in a while, I'm not listening carefully to see if I hear Yamir in the background. Okay, I'm listening for that a little, but not that much.

"Evan's mom is gonna pick me up. She can pick you up too, if you want."

"Sure," I say. For some reason, it didn't occur to me that Evan would be there. I don't know why. He's friends with Travis and Gavin, so it makes sense. Plus, he's Sunny's boyfriend. But as soon as Sunny mentions him, my stomach goes knotty. What if Sunny spends the whole time with him? The AGE girls have each other and don't really need me. And Zoe and Erica will be joined at the hip.

I don't know who I'll hang out with.

Travis will probably pay attention to me, because he always does. And I like it, sometimes. But not all the time. I'm scared we'll get left alone together and I won't know what to do or what to say. Some days I like him. And I think I can *like* him, like him. But other days I'm not sure and I just miss Yamir.

My acting like I don't care about Yamir is just that, acting. Of course I care. I just can't admit that to anyone.

I wonder if I'll ever get so into this acting thing that I'll forget how I really feel.

I doubt it.

Evan's mom picks me up, and I say good-bye to Mom and Grandma. They don't seem worried about me going to a party the way they used to worry about Claudia. I wonder why. Maybe they trust me more. Or maybe it's because I'm not in high school yet.

I guess they're saving all their worrying for next year.

"Hi, Lucy." Evan's mom smiles back at me from the front seat. "So nice to see you."

"Likewise," I reply, because it's something my mom always says.

Sunny cracks up, of course. "Lucy is now forty years old."

I hit her on the arm, but then I start laughing too. I knew she'd say something like that. She's so predictable.

Evan's sitting in the front seat, and his hair is all glossy from some kind of gel. It smells really strong too, like a combination of men's cologne and the gardenia-scented counter cleaner my mom uses. I open my window a tiny crack, even though it's cold outside.

"So, Dad's going to pick you guys up," Evan's mom tells him. "What time?"

"No idea," he replies. "I'll call you."

Evan's been surprisingly quiet this whole ride. Maybe he's nervous. He's never been to a party like this either, probably. At least not with Sunny. He's probably freaked out that they'll have to play some kind of game like Truth or Dare or Five Minutes in Heaven.

Come to think of it, I'm scared of that too.

I start to come up with escape plans. I can say that I have a stomachache. Or that there's a pharmacy emergency and I need to help. No one will believe the second one, but at least it's something to have on the list in case I get really desperate.

"Thanks for the ride," I say as I'm getting out of the car. I immediately try to think of what my mom, grandma, and dad are doing tonight. Grandma was going to the movies with her friend Flo. Mom didn't say, and I'm not sure what Dad's doing. I hope one of them is available to pick me up.

As soon as I'm on the front steps of Travis's house, I immediately want to leave. I feel like Sunny at the mall last year, before she started going out with Evan. She liked him but couldn't handle being around him.

Maybe this means I like Travis. Maybe I've liked him all this time and didn't even realize it.

I totally confuse myself.

18

Lucy's tip for surviving eighth grade:
Don't compare yourself to others.

The door is open and we walk into the twins' house. Their parents are sitting in the living room reading. They don't say hi. They look up and smile, but that's it.

They don't tell us where the party is, but we see a sign that says PARTY DOWNSTAIRS.

With each step I take toward the basement, I become sweatier, my stomach gets knottier, and I feel more and more like I'm about to throw up.

This isn't good.

"Are you okay?" Sunny asks. "You look clammy."

"I do?" Oh no. I may feel clammy, but I don't want to look clammy. "Actually, I'm gonna hit the bathroom. Will you wait for me?"

She nods but seems reluctant, like she's anxious to get downstairs. Evan says he'll meet us down there, and I immediately feel relieved. I need a few minutes alone with my best friend. That will fix everything.

"What's wrong with you?" Sunny whispers when we go into the bathroom together.

"I don't know. This just feels so, I don't know, mature, and so different from the stuff we usually do."

"Come on, Luce. We're in a basement in Old Mill with kids in our grade."

"Right." I don't want to go into all the reasons why I'm nervous, because I think that will just make me more nervous. I touch up my makeup, patting some concealer on my chin and reapplying my lip gloss. Even this little touch-up relaxes me. I take a deep breath. I give myself a cold, hard stare in the mirror.

Lucy, you can do this.

Sunny and I go downstairs, and there are already so many people there. It's not our whole grade, but it's close. The basement is big—pretty much the whole length and width of their house. And they have a big house. Maybe one of the biggest houses I've ever seen in Old Mill.

The AGE girls are sitting on the blue velvet couch in the corner, looking at their phones and sipping cans of soda. Erica and Zoe are standing in the other corner with their arms folded across their chests.

Where to start? I wonder. I remind myself of my mission: to help Zoe and Gavin get together, and to make the AGE girls enjoy themselves for the first time in their lives.

I can do it. And if I focus on everyone else, I won't have time to think about my own worries and fears. Having a mission helps me calm down. It gives me a sense of purpose.

"I'm gonna go over to the foosball table with Evan," Sunny says. She squeezes my arm. "Are you okay?"

I nod. I can't hold Sunny back. In my heart of hearts, I wish she would stay by my side the whole night, but I know that's not fair.

I don't want to stand alone at this party. When you stand alone, you feel like everyone notices that you're alone. Claudia has told me so many times that no one is really paying attention. But it's still hard to accept that. When I'm alone, I feel like there's a flashing neon sign above my head: LUCY DESBERG IS ALONE RIGHT NOW.

"Lucy!" Travis runs over to me and hands me a can of soda. "So pumped you're here."

He's wearing a long-sleeved polo with the collar up a little, and just like Evan his hair is glossed and spiky, with only one strand that won't stay where he wants it. He keeps pushing it back, but it repeatedly falls and lands in the middle of his forehead. I have to stop looking at it.

"Come. I want to show you our man cave."

Man cave? I've never heard a kid call a room a man cave. But I don't say anything, just follow him.

There's a whole separate room in the back of the basement. From the outside it looks like a closet. My stomach swirls around like a bug in a glass of lemonade. It's going to be one of those awkward scenes from a TV show.

He even takes my hand. It seems like we're the only ones at this party right now. How did we go from two people who talked occasionally before the start of band to two people alone in a basement?

"This is it," he says as he turns on the light.

We're not in a closet. We're in a giant room with a pool table and pinball machine. It also has an orange leather couch and high tables that look like leaves. It almost seems like a lounge in a swanky hotel.

"Cool." I smile. "Really cool."

I need to come up with an excuse to get out of here. Maybe I'm hungry? I saw some chips on the table in the other room.

"Thanks," he says. I feel him looking at me, but I don't make eye contact. If I make eye contact, it's all over.

"Why isn't anyone hanging out in here?" I ask. "It's so cool. Everyone is crowded in the other room."

"We're gonna open it up soon." He slicks his hair back for the millionth time. "I wanted to show you first."

"Really?" I ask. That feels too big, too important. I don't want to be that important to Travis.

Maybe that's how you know if you like someone. If you don't want to be the most important person in the world to that person, you're probably not that interested in going out with them.

"Come on, let's go tell everyone to come in," he says. He makes it sound like we're hosting the party together. But I don't really care. I'm just grateful to leave this room and take a break from being alone with him for a few minutes.

I follow him and, thankfully, he doesn't grab my hand again.

We're back in the other room for two seconds when Erica and Zoe run up to me. Travis says that he's going to check on the sodas and he'll see me soon.

"We have to talk to you," Erica says as soon as Travis is gone. "Privately."

This can't be good.

"What is it?" I ask, when we're in the back corner near the tall gray armchair.

"You're a sneak," Erica says. "Going into another room alone with Travis. What about Yamir?"

"Nothing is happening with Travis," I say. "We're friends."
I force myself not to laugh. Erica acts like she's on a reality TV
show.

It occurs to me that I should probably say the opposite—
that nothing is happening with Yamir. That we don't talk at
all. That he's probably going out with that girl Sienna. That's
the real truth.

But I can't bring myself to say that. I can't even bring
myself to think that.

"Anyway," I continue, "let's talk about more important
things. Like Zoe and Gavin." I pause, and a genius idea comes
to me out of the blue. "And who Erica should go to the Masquerade with. We need to find you someone awesome."

Erica rolls her eyes. "Oh Lordy. Lucy Desberg is my
matchmaker now?"

"She's been doing a good job for me," Zoe admits.

"Well, if you don't want my help, that's fine too." I smile
at Erica as sweetly as I can. It's taken me eight years, but I
finally know how to handle Erica Crane. That is a major
accomplishment.

"Fine." Erica folds her arms across her chest. "But if you
don't like Travis, then maybe I will. Zoe and I are BFFs, and
it only makes sense that we have twin brothers for our boyfriends."

She kind of has a point. Maybe if I set Erica up with Travis, I'll feel better.

I think about that for a second. On the one hand, it's nice to have Travis's attention. On the other hand, it's so stressful. But on a third hand, Travis is a nice guy, and Erica Crane is . . . Erica Crane.

There has to be an answer.

"Let's just see how the party goes," I say. "We don't know who else is going to show up. The whole night is ahead of us."

Saying that gives me a sense of hope and excitement—combined with a sense of dread and fear. I guess that's how I feel about life right now. Life as an eighth grader who will soon be in high school.

I planned for it all to be perfect and the best time ever, yet it's a box of assorted emotions, changing every other day.

"Great idea," Zoe says. "Now, where's Gavin?"

19

Lucy's tip for surviving eighth grade:
Try to think about things from other
people's perspectives.

Everyone starts to shuffle into the "man cave"—which is pretty much just a game room. Someone wheels the foosball table in there too. Some boys are playing pool, and the AGE girls are involved in an intense game of foosball. I can't tell if they know how to play or if they're just goofing off.

I spot Gavin coming down the stairs carrying a tray of mini hot dogs. "There he is," I whisper to Zoe. He looks like a waiter at a fancy party, only he's not wearing a black bow tie.

Zoe straightens her hair and folds her arms across her chest.

"Don't stand like that," I whisper. "It looks like you're closed off and unapproachable."

"Huh?" she whispers.

"I read it in a magazine once."

Erica whispers something into Zoe's other ear that I can't hear.

"I'll go get a mini hot dog and tell Gavin to come hang with us," I suggest. "Just wait here. Look like you're involved in a conversation and Erica's saying something really funny."

As I carefully walk over to where Gavin's standing at the foot of the stairs, I try to avoid eye contact with anyone. At the same time I'm trying to spot Travis, so that he can't swoop in and suggest we hang out alone again.

"I love mini hot dogs," I tell Gavin when I get to him.

"Take a plate!"

There's something about this party that makes it seem like Travis and Gavin are professional party throwers. There have to be at least seventy-five kids in this basement, but no one seems stressed. Not even their parents.

"Erica and Zoe want some too. I can't carry that many." I make a sort of damsel-in-distress face, which is a little lame, but I think it'll get Gavin over to where Zoe's standing. "Will you bring the tray over there?" I smile.

"At your service, madam!" He follows me over to the corner behind the pool table.

"Don't worry, guys, I've brought the hot-dog man over to you!" I say, and laugh, but no one else does. Maybe it wasn't that funny.

"Lucy is the hot-dog expert," Erica says. "You know how she won that hot-dog-eating contest last summer. Right, Gavin?"

People bring up that hot-dog contest way more often than I thought they would.

"Yeah. Pretty impressive." Gavin nods. "I'd high-five you, but I'd probably drop the tray."

"Thanks. If the party gets slow, we can always start an impromptu mini-hot-dog-eating contest," I suggest. "Just an idea."

"Then people will barf all over their basement." Erica totally shoots down my idea.

I ignore her comment. "So, Gavin, are you and Zoe in any classes together?"

He thinks for a second. "Hmm. Maybe chorus?"

"Oh yeah." Zoe smiles.

"But social studies too. Remember the rap?" I realize it probably seems odd that I know about that, so I add, "Sunny thought it was so funny. She had to tell me about it."

"Duh!" Gavin puts down the tray and hits himself on the head. "Obviously. How did I forget?"

Soon they're involved in a conversation about their rap performance, and I say loudly, "Erica, come with me for a second. I want to show you something in the other room."

At first she looks confused, but then she gets it.

"Zoe cannot have a boyfriend or date for the Masquerade before I do," Erica says on our way to the other room. "Do not let that happen. Do you understand how serious this is?"

"I do." But I don't—not really. She should be capable of being happy for her friend. I forgot how competitive Erica Crane can be.

"Do you understand?" she asks again.

I nod slowly. This might be an example of the whole "no good deed goes unpunished" thing. But it's too soon to tell.

"Come on. Let's sit on those couches over there," I say. I think better when I'm seated. And I kind of want to hide from Travis. Also, where's Sunny? I haven't seen her or Evan in what feels like hours.

When we're seated I ask Erica if she likes anyone, of if she has anyone in mind for her date.

"Not really," she says. "All the boys in our grade are immature or boring. I want a high school boy."

"Oh."

"That's why I need you, Lucy." She glares at me. "I know you're playing down the whole Yamir thing. But I also know you guys are in love and will get married."

"Really?" Erica sounds like she knows more about my future than I do—and I really want to believe her.

"Totally. It's like a classic love story. Childhood friends. You grew up together. The whole girl-next-door thing."

"I'm not sure that means anything."

She rolls her eyes. "Whatever. Just trust me. You're getting married. Now tell Yamir to find me a cool high school boyfriend."

"Okay. I will."

"Now, I mean." She picks up my bag, about to open it. "Where's your phone? Text him now."

"Huh? No. I'll just talk to him when I see him."

"Text him now, or I'll go tell Travis that you're in love with him and you don't care about Yamir." Right now Erica seems like some crazed monster you'd see in an animated movie. She's a wild animal looking for her prey. "Do it, Lucy. I mean it."

I have no idea what to do. When Erica Crane tells you to do something, you pretty much have to do it. But maybe this won't be so bad. It gives me an excuse to text Yamir. Sure, it contradicts my whole not-caring attitude. But this is for Erica, not for me.

And he knows how scary she is.

"Fine." I dig to the bottom of my bag and find my phone. No texts. No e-mails. No calls. Claudia has been missing for days. As soon as I get home, I'm telling Mom and Grandma. It's starting to really worry me.

I sift through my text messages to find the last one from Yamir.

All it says is *fart*, and it's from four weeks ago. So there's that.

Hey. Erica Crane wants you to find her a high
school boyfriend. Get on that.

I show her the text before I send it.

"Good work."

"Now what?" I ask.

"Let's just sit and see if he responds. I'll go get us some
sodas."

I want to tell her to come back quickly, but that sounds
needy and desperate, so I don't. I sit here and stare at my phone,
half because I'm worried about Yamir writing back and half
because I don't want to look like a loser sitting alone.

"You okay?" Travis seems to come out of nowhere. He sits
down next to me. I quickly shove my phone in my bag. The
last thing I need is a text from Yamir to pop up while Travis is
talking to me.

"Oh yeah. Fine." I smile. "Just digesting the mini hot dogs." I
have absolutely no idea how I come up with half the things I say.

"They're delicious," he says.

And then I can't think of anything else to say.

He says, "I have something cool to show you."

My stomach sinks. He's going to take me somewhere alone
again. I can feel it. I try to think of an excuse, somewhere I have
to go. Or maybe say that Erica will be back soon with our sodas.

But I see her in the game room talking to Zoe and Gavin again, holding cans of Sprite. She's not coming back anytime soon.

"Come with me," he says when I don't respond.

"What is it?" Maybe if I know what it is and where we're going, I won't feel as nervous.

"You'll see," he says.

On the way to wherever we're going, I give Erica and Zoe looks. Confused looks. But they just smile like everything is awesome.

We walk back through the game room, up two steps, and into another room. Travis flicks on a switch, and I gasp.

"You have a planetarium in your house?" I ask, shocked.

"Apparently!" He fiddles with some settings and changes the lighting, so it's pitch-black with a zillion stars on the ceiling. We can't hear anything going on in the other room. It seems like we're a million miles away from anyone. "The previous owners of the house were astronomers. I guess they were really obsessed with the planets and the stars and needed to have access to them all the time. My parents looked into converting it to a home gym, but Gavin and I begged them to keep it."

"Yeah! This is way cooler than a home gym!"

"Come here." He points to a row of seats like in a movie theater. "I'll show you how cool this is."

My rumbling stomach starts to calm down, and I sit in

one of the red velvet armchairs. Travis has a giant remote in his hand, and I wonder if he knows what he's doing or if he's just pushing buttons. Probably a little of both.

"This is a real planetarium," I say. "Like the one in New York, just with fewer seats."

"I've never been there, but I believe you." He's quiet for a few minutes while he figures out which buttons to push. "Here, check this out."

The stars on the ceiling disappear, but now we see the whole solar system in intricate detail—every crevice on every planet—and he can zoom in so we can look at each one, like we're literally standing over it. There's even a setting you can switch to that has a woman's voice narrating a guide to the solar system. There's also a sound-track setting that plays soothing music as the stars twinkle. And our chairs go back, so we're almost lying flat. It's one of the most amazing things I've ever seen.

I'm so busy looking at the ceiling that I'm caught 100 percent off guard when it happens.

Travis kisses me. Just a quick peck—but it feels wrong. All wrong.

I pull away. "Oh, um . . ."

"What? Sorry. Was that not okay?" I can't see his face but I bet it's all crumpled. The way he looks after he has to play a solo in band and messes up too many notes.

"Oh, it's just that, um." I stop. I have no idea how to say this. Should I tell him about Yamir? Is there really anything to tell?

"What?" he asks again.

"I just wasn't expecting that," I tell him, which is a lie. I was expecting it, just not at that second.

"We don't have to," he says.

"Let's wait." I look at him, but we can't see each other. Maybe it's better that way.

"Okay." He pushes another button and changes the setting to have the stars spread out in a different way. "I don't know what I'm doing anyway."

For some reason that makes me feel better.

We stay in the planetarium for a little while longer, and for a few minutes I forget about the party. I forget about my text to Yamir. I forget about everything.

Right now it's just Travis and me and a zillion stars.

And I don't know how I feel about that.

Lucy's tip for surviving eighth grade:
Accept the fact that you will make mistakes.

A few minutes after we leave the planetarium, I find Sunny and Evan by the jukebox.

"Where have you been?" she mutters.

"I'll explain later."

"Well, something happened with Erica Crane and your phone," she says. "And now my brother's coming here. With Clint, Anthony, and some new kid, Elias."

"What?"

"That's all I know, Lucy." She shakes her head, looking frustrated.

I go to find Erica, and on the way I notice that I left my bag on the couch. I guess I was so nervous about going off alone with Travis that I forgot it. I find my phone and discover that Erica was texting Yamir. From my phone. Pretending to be me.

Sweetie, bring someone cute for Erica.

Sweetie? I would never call him that.

Right now? Where r u? U are being so weird.

She texted back the twins' address and everything.

Fine. We're just sitting here playing Xbox. We'll come.

So it wasn't really me texting him. And he doesn't seem that excited about it. But he's coming. That has to mean he wants to see me. Right?

I'm on my way to find Erica and yell at her for going through my bag and texting Yamir, but it's too late.

They're already here.

"I can't believe you dragged us to a middle school party," Yamir says when he sees me.

I sniff. "*Hello* would be a nicer way to greet me."

"Hello," he grumbles.

Erica comes over to us. She's holding a glass of fruit punch. I wonder if she knows that her lips are hot pink.

Yamir nods in her direction and then looks back at Elias. "Elias, this is Erica," he says, lazily. "Erica, this is Elias."

"Hi, I'm Lucy," I say to him, since Yamir clearly doesn't care about introducing me.

"Hey." This Elias kid can't be what Erica had in mind. At least, I don't think so. He has hair so blond it looks bleached. And the chubbiest cheeks I've ever seen. He has a baby face but in a high schooler's body. A young high schooler's body.

"Did you just move here?" I ask.

"No, not really. We live in West Seaside but my mom teaches at Old Mill High School, so she got me rezoned."

"I see."

I guess I'm wrong about Erica's taste, though, because she seems at least a little bit interested. "Follow me, Elias. Let me show you around," she says, like this is her house.

Clint and Anthony go to play foosball, and Yamir and I are left standing by ourselves.

"Do you want to sit?" I ask. I want to tell him about the planetarium, but then I realize I shouldn't. I probably don't need to go into the fact that Travis and I were in a dark room alone together and that he kissed me.

"Yeah, sure." He looks at his phone and follows me to the couches where Erica and I were sitting before.

We're chatting about nothing all that important—soccer,

his parents' upcoming trip to India, a new taco at Dream Tacos—when he turns to me and says, "So, what's up with you and that Travis kid?"

"Shouldn't I be asking you the same thing?"

"Me and Travis?" He laughs.

"No, okay, not the same exact thing." I look at him with his long eyelashes and a strand of thick hair falling in his left eye. Do I really want to say this? It could ruin everything.

But everything's pretty much ruined already.

I take a deep breath. "You and Sienna."

"Sienna?" he echoes.

"Yeah, that girl you seem to be with all the time. The pretty one from Westport."

"Oh, you mean the girl I have to tutor in science because she moved and is behind?"

"Oh. Okay."

I'm quiet now. I shouldn't have started this.

"So, your turn. You and Travis. The kid who lives in this house. Who threw this party. Who just took you alone into his planetarium."

He knows about the planetarium. There isn't that much to know. But he knows it.

"Nothing is going on. But I don't know why you'd care. You obviously don't like me anymore."

"What are you talking about?" He seems genuinely confused, but that doesn't make sense.

"You don't call me, or e-mail, or text, or anything, Yamir. The last text you sent was four weeks ago, and all it said was *fart*." I can't look at him right now. His thigh is touching my thigh, but I can't look at him. "You don't act like you like me. You don't act like you want to be my boyfriend. You don't care at all."

"Thanks for telling me what I care about," he says. "Clearly you didn't care enough to talk to me about it. You were just going to forget everything that ever happened and move on to someone else."

All around us people are laughing and talking and there's music playing. But right here, on this couch, it feels like the world is ending.

"That's not what happened," I mumble. "I tried to talk to you that night when I slept over. But nothing changed. And you ignored me at Sushi of Gari. It was all so obvious. I just didn't think I should spend so much time caring about you."

He looks at me, finally. "I see," he says. "Let's just move on, then."

"Yamir, you don't care about me. Admit it. Maybe in a friend way, but that's it. It's obvious. If you liked me, you wouldn't treat me like this. Why can't you just say it?"

He takes one long look at me. "I'm sorry you feel that way."

That's the dumbest expression in the world. So what if he's sorry that I feel that way? It's not like he's going to do anything about it.

He gets up from the couch and walks over to Clint and Anthony. They look back at me, and then the three of them keep walking. I guess they're leaving. But it looks like Elias is staying here. He and Erica haven't stopped talking since the moment he got here.

At least there's that.

21

Lucy's tip for surviving eighth grade:
Try not to obsess about things you have no control over.

It feels like I have to walk through humid, smoky air for the rest of the weekend. In reality, it's freezing and snowing off and on, but I can't seem to move gracefully. I feel stuck. Like I'm pushing through walls of thick cement.

On Sunday morning I wake up and the first thing I do is check my phone, hoping for something from Yamir. A conversation at a party can't be the end. Right? I mean, there has to be more to our story.

But Yamir hasn't gotten in touch.

I'm staring at my phone, willing it to ring or buzz or something—and it actually does.

But it's not Yamir. It's Claudia.

"Where have you been, Claud?" I shriek.

"Oh, Luce. I don't even know where to start."

"What?" I immediately assume some crazy person has kidnapped her and locked her in a basement for weeks.

"I'll explain soon," she says.

"Just start now. I've been so worried."

"My phone's dying," she tells me. "Alert Mom and Grandma. I'll be there in an hour."

She'll be here in an hour?

Great. Now I have the job of telling Mom and Grandma that something's wrong with Claudia.

I lie in bed for a few more minutes. Maybe if I go back to sleep, I'll wake up and this will all be a dream. Or more of a nightmare, I guess.

But no luck. I'm up.

Downstairs, Mom and Grandma are still sitting at the kitchen table sharing a *New York Times*, a carafe of coffee, and a basket of homemade blueberry muffins. If I wasn't brokenhearted about Yamir and freaked out about Claudia, I would be 100 percent in love with this picture.

"Good morning, sleepyhead," Mom says, pulling out a chair for me.

Ever since the spa opened and business has turned around, Mom and Grandma take Sundays off. They don't take it for granted either—they always make special breakfasts and lounge in their pajamas for as long as they can.

"What's wrong?" Grandma says as soon as she sees me. Either I'm a bad actress or Grandma knows me better than anyone else. She always seems to sense when something is up.

"Well. Where to start?"

They both look at me.

"I guess I should let you know that Claudia will be here in an hour."

"What? Oh Lord!" Grandma holds her head. "She flunked out of school. I knew it, Jane. She has not been serious enough about her studies."

In a way I feel better. Maybe that's all it is. I was thinking something much worse, like she'd been arrested.

"Maybe it's good news, Ma. Ever think of that?"

My mom does have a point. Does Claudia play the lottery? Or maybe she won some kind of award. Who knows.

Grandma shakes her head. "I doubt it. Good news is usually first delivered over the telephone. And besides—why is she spending money on a flight?"

"Ma! Enough. We're doing fine with money now. You sound like someone who lived through the Depression!"

They go back and forth like this for a few minutes while I pick at a blueberry muffin. I'm not going to tell them about Yamir. They don't need something else to be upset about. And besides, I don't know if I want their advice.

I stare at the clock waiting for something to happen. I know we all assumed that Claudia flew home, but maybe she didn't. Maybe that girl Lauren drove her again. Maybe she took the train. There are so many possibilities.

I'm reading one of the *Times* Sunday wedding stories when my phone buzzes. I'm grateful for the distraction. People with broken hearts shouldn't be reading stories about weddings.

"How are you?" Sunny asks in a very serious voice. She must know.

"Fine, I guess."

"*Soooo*, Yamir punched a hole in the wall," she says. "I don't think you can say he doesn't care."

"He told you I said that?" I ask.

"Yeah. But that's pretty much all he said." She stops talking for a few seconds, and it feels like an hour has passed. "Did something happen with Travis?"

"No! I mean, yes and no." I walk out of the room and upstairs. "He tried to kiss me. And maybe our lips touched. But it wasn't my idea. And then we stopped."

"Oh."

It's quiet again. I can't tell what's happening. It seems like Sunny is mad at me, but that doesn't make any sense.

"Where were you and Evan? I didn't see you guys the whole night."

She says, "We can discuss that later," and then she's quiet again. "I gotta go, Luce. Sorry all of this happened."

That's it? I don't get it. I need Sunny now more than ever, but she seems to think this is my fault.

A minute after we hang up, my phone rings again, from a random Connecticut number. I figure it's Claudia calling from someone else's phone or something, so I answer it.

"Lucy," a girl says on the other end.

"Yeah?"

I have no idea who it is.

"So, that kid Elias is awesome," the girl says.

Oh. Now I know who it is. Erica Crane. She must be calling from her landline.

"He is?" I ask.

"Yeah. He knows about all these obscure bands and he's really into music. Plus, he seems, like, way older. Like way, way older than all the guys we know."

"Um, that's great."

I don't understand this call. It almost seems like Erica is thanking me, but that's so not like her.

"But I heard about you and Yamir. And that really stinks."

"Yeah, thanks. I'm really upset and—"

She interrupts. "I need you to fix it. Say you're sorry or

whatever. Because we need to go on double dates. Elias is in high school, and I can't make this happen all on my own."

Oh. So that's why she's calling.

"It's not really up to me. Yamir has been ignoring me for a long time."

"Really? You made him sound all amazing," she says. "So you're a liar too?"

Ouch. That was harsh. I don't even know what to say.

"I'd suggest you find a way to fix it," she warns. "Or soon everyone will know you're a liar. You don't want that, do you?"

"Erica, come on," I plead. "You don't know the whole story."

"True. And I don't really care about the story," she says. "Just fix it. Bye."

Okay, so somehow this morning has gone from bad to worse, and Claudia's not even here yet. I pray that Mom's right, that Claudia is coming home with good news. I'm not sure I can take any more bad news.

22

Lucy's tip for surviving eighth grade:
Spend time with your family. It can help.

An hour has passed and Claudia's still not here. I think she said an hour, but maybe she said a few hours. I don't know.

My mind is spinning with all the horrible things happening: Yamir and I breaking up, Claudia's mystery trip, Sunny being annoyed with me, pressure from Erica. I need to talk to someone, and there's only one person I can think of.

"Evan, hey, it's Lucy," I say, as soon as he answers.

"Hey!"

"Listen, I hope it's not weird that I'm calling you, but after our chat at the beach, I really think you might give the best advice."

He laughs. "Well, thanks."

I sit back on my bed, and try to even out the feathers in

my down comforter. "Everything felt crazy at the party last night. Didn't it?"

"What do you mean?" He asks in a way that sounds like he's actually interested in the response.

"I mean, the whole thing with Yamir showing up, and Erica and Elias, and now I think Sunny's mad at me."

I wait for him to say something, but he's quiet for a few seconds. Maybe it was a mistake to call him.

"Lucy, you always get worked up over this stuff, and then it's fixed in, like, a day," he tells me. "Just go with the flow."

I don't even know what that means. It sounds like good advice. But also like something to say when you can't think of anything else.

"Yeah."

"Yamir is obviously confused. So let him work out his stuff."

Again, it sounds good, but is he really saying anything?

"You and Sunny are the perfect couple. How do you do it?" I ask. I hear all kinds of noise coming from my mom's room. Things dropping. Doors closing. Exasperated groans. I have no idea what's happening out there.

"I don't know, I guess we're just awesome," he says. "You shouldn't compare your relationship to ours, though. Everybody's different."

"Uh-huh."

"Look," he says. "Travis likes you. Yamir's been a little bit of a doofus lately. So just go with it. And who cares about Erica? She's never going to be nice."

"Maybe she's on a path to being nicer," I say.

"No, she's not."

"All right. Well, thanks, Evan," I say. "You can tell Sunny I called you. I don't want her to think I'm going behind her back or anything, or that she's been replaced by you!"

"Okay, I gotcha." He pauses, and in the background I hear the screeching-tire sounds of some kind of car video game. I guess he was multitasking. "Catch you later."

I end the call and wonder if I feel any better than before I called him. Maybe a little. Maybe not. I guess I don't feel any worse.

I walk downstairs to grab some kind of a snack. Stress eating is hard to avoid on days like this.

Mom is in the foyer, putting her coat on. "I have to go," she says.

"What? No. You can't go. Claudia will be here soon." I decide to sit on the bench by the front door so I'll be able to see Claudia when she comes.

"Don't even ask. Adrienne had some kind of problem with the pet sitter she lined up and now she's in a bind, and I need to go over and check on the animals every day this week. Apparently in addition to the cats, she has two birds now. The animals have been alone for three days already."

"*Eww*. Gross." That explains all the crashing and banging I heard before. My mom always drops stuff when she's in a hurry.

She makes a face. "I know."

We are not cat people. Or bird people.

Mom should be more put out by this. It's making me even madder that she's not as angry as I am.

"Where'd your mother go?" Grandma asks, coming down the stairs.

"Adrienne. She needs someone to check on her cats and birds."

"Your mother does not know how to say no." Grandma sits down next to me, and we look out the window together. "She's left us to deal with your sister alone, I guess."

"Apparently."

We sit there quietly for a few more minutes and then Grandma says to me, "You sure it's only your sister that's troubling you?"

I shrug. "I don't know."

"I see. It's okay to not know."

Grandma's usually pretty comforting, but I don't feel like

having some kind of deep discussion. Not when everything's falling apart.

If I don't figure out how to make Erica happy, everyone will know that I haven't been honest about Yamir. The AGE girls will know I lied to them.

Eighth-Grade Masquerade is in a month, and my life is a complete disaster. I think I'm better at handling grown-up problems. Eighth-grade problems seem much, much harder.

I should never have attempted a perfect last semester. A merely okay semester would have been a lofty enough goal.

Lucy's tip for surviving eighth grade:
Be open to surprises.

An Old Mill taxi pulls into our driveway, and Grandma and I leap up from the couch. We're outside on the porch waiting for Claudia before she's even gotten out of the car.

I'm having déjà vu back to last summer when Claudia pulled up with Lauren and Bean. Only a million things are different now: Claudia's getting out of a taxi, not Lauren's car. It's freezing outside. And Yamir's not sitting on the porch taking pictures.

I want to go back to that moment. Sometimes I wish that life could be like the photo stream on my phone. You could click back and forth from one moment to another. You could revisit happier times and take a break from harder ones.

"*Hiiii,*" Claudia says, running up the steps to the porch.

She reaches out to hug both of us at the same time. I guess she's not staying long, because she only has a small bag with her.

"Let's go in. I'm freezing," she says. She's the only one of the three of us with a coat on, plus she's coming from Chicago. She should be used to cold weather.

She drops her bag by the front door and hangs her coat on the coat tree. She walks into the kitchen like she's been here for weeks, like nothing unusual is happening. She grabs an apple from the bowl and fills up a glass of water.

It's the strangest thing. It's like she has no idea we're ridiculously worried and curious about why she's here.

Grandma goes back into the living room and picks up her book. I sit next to her and wait. I'm not going to interrogate Claudia. I'll wait until she's ready to talk.

"So," she starts, and sits down on the brown armchair across from Grandma.

"I'm going to guess you weren't arrested," I say. "You seem too calm for someone who might be heading to jail."

"Very funny, Luce."

"Start talking," Grandma says to Claudia. "You don't just appear out of nowhere like this."

If Mom were here, she'd probably yell at Grandma for saying something like that, but I stay quiet. I kind of want to see how Claudia explains this. And sometimes a little tough love is helpful.

"Where's Mom?" Claudia asks.

I tell her about "the bind" Adrienne is in. "She needs someone to check in on the cats and the birds. Sounds like she has a whole pet store in her house."

"Yuck," is all Claudia says.

"Claudia. Come on. What's going on?" Grandma seems frustrated that Claudia isn't getting to the point.

"Well, I came for advice." She looks down at her feet. "Bean asked me to marry him!"

"What?" Grandma screams and stands up. "Claudia Desberg. Stop this right now."

I can't say I'm totally surprised. It could be worse. She could already be married. Oh no! Maybe she is.

I stand up too. "Wait? You didn't answer him, right?"

Claudia's the only one still sitting down, and it feels funny. "Great to know you both love Bean." She half-smiles.

"This is not about loving Bean or not loving Bean," Grandma says, sitting down again, so I follow along. "This is about the fact that you're barely twenty years old. And you're not getting married. It's not even legal!"

"Actually it's totally legal," Claudia replies. "I think. I'd have to look it up. Whatever."

Grandma shakes her head like she's in pain. "Tell us the whole story, Claudia. Please don't leave out any important information."

Under her breath I hear Grandma add, "You girls are so much like your mother. It kills me."

We both ignore her, even though we know she wanted us to hear that.

"Well, okay, I should clarify," Claudia continues. "He didn't ask me to marry him *right now*. It wasn't like that. He just has this whole plan for us to travel and live abroad for a few years after college, and he thinks it's better if we're married."

"No. The answer is no. You cannot get married!" Grandma stands up again, and I almost start laughing. It feels like she's been up and down a million times. This time she leaves the room. We hear her stomp up the stairs, and even though she's not much of a door slammer, we hear her bedroom door close forcefully.

"So, that wasn't a success," Claudia says, laughing a little.

"Of course it wasn't," I say. For a smart girl, Claudia can be really, really dumb. "You didn't think she'd be happy about it, did you?"

"Um, I guess not. But I thought Mom would be here to sort of help."

"Well, blame the cats."

"She has birds now too. But, of course. We can blame most things on cats."

We both start cracking up, and it feels good to laugh. There are a million problems lingering, but sometimes you have to laugh anyway. Laugh in spite of all the problems.

Mom gets home a little while later. Her hair is tied up in a messy bun and she looks disheveled.

"What happened?" I ask, turning off the TV.

"One of the cats had some stomach troubles," she says. "Don't even ask."

"I won't. I don't want to know."

"Did Claudia ever get home?"

I nod. "Yeah. You might want to go talk to Grandma."

Mom clenches her teeth. "That bad, huh?"

"Oh yeah."

"Where is she?" Mom puts her hands on her hips like she's about to take control. The thing is, she's not good at being in charge. It's actually kind of funny to watch.

"In her room, I guess."

I keep the TV off, because I want to hear what happens. The thing that confuses me is that I'm not sure if Claudia came home to ask permission, or to get our opinion, or what. I'm not even sure why she came home. I guess getting engaged worried her in some way. She must know it's absolutely insane.

I hear voices but I can't make out what's being said. I leave the den and tiptoe up the stairs. I'll hang out in my room with the door open, and then I'll be able to hear everything.

"Claudia, you can't make a decision for two years from now!" Grandma yells. "That is absurd. And he's nuts to expect that of you."

"How many times have I said he didn't want an answer right away?" Claudia says.

"So then why exactly did you fly home?" Mom asks. "I'm thrilled to see you. Don't get me wrong. But why the urgency? Why does this need to be decided or discussed right now?"

There's silence for a few moments. And then Claudia says, "I guess it startled me. I wanted a break from everyone at school. I wanted to talk with you guys. But you get so crazy. Everything becomes a fight."

Then she starts crying.

"It's not a fight, Claud," Mom says in her soft, trying-to-be-comforting voice. "We just want what's best. And it doesn't make sense to make these decisions when you're so young."

"Because look at what happened to you," Claudia says, and something about her voice makes it clear she already regrets saying it.

"No," Mom replies. "I have no regrets."

"Jane, please," Grandma sneers. "Frankly, Claudia, I think you need a break from Bean. You've been together since the first day of college, and it seems like he's getting ahead of himself. Take time for yourself. Meet other boys."

No one responds to that.

A few seconds later Claudia says, "Well, Mia's home for her grandparents' anniversary party this weekend, so we're going to grab some coffee. Can I borrow the car?"

"Be home for dinner," Mom says. "And tell Mia we say hi."

Claudia comes into my room before she goes. "They're crazy," she whispers.

I don't know if I agree. I mean, yeah, sometimes they're a little hard to take. But in this case I think Bean is the crazy one.

When I don't respond to that, she says, "So, what's new with you, Luce? How's Yamir?"

I'm faced with a choice: tell her the truth, because she's my sister. Or lie to her, like I've been lying to everyone else. It becomes surprisingly easy to lie when you've been doing it so consistently for so long.

"He's okay," I say. Technically that's not really a lie, but it's not saying much of the truth.

She checks herself out in the mirror above my dresser and smears on some of my lip gloss. "Things are good with you two?"

"Well, I can't really say that," I reply. It turns out I can't lie to my sister. I mean, I did sort of kiss someone else last night, and Yamir and I broke up.

"What do you mean?" Claudia turns around, sounding shocked. "Clearly you need to fill me in," she says. "But I'm almost late to meet Mia. Talk later?"

I nod.

Claudia goes out, and the house is quiet again. I think about the conversation Claudia had with Mom and Grandma, and it makes me wonder if she's telling the truth. It feels like something's missing from the story. Maybe she's scared to go into more detail because Mom and Grandma get so intense.

Maybe we're all only telling half the story all the time.

I guess it makes us feel safer that way. We can't reveal everything or we'll be vulnerable. If we tell our stories in bits and pieces, there's time to see how people will respond, time for us to adjust what we say as we go.

There has to be more to this. Bean's not crazy. And Claudia hates to leave school, even for a few days.

I told everyone that things were great with Yamir for so long when they really weren't so great. I did it because it was easier at the time. But it was just putting off the hard part.

I guess the hard part comes eventually, no matter what you do.

Lucy's tip for surviving eighth grade:
Be honest. Always be honest.

@laudia isn't flying back the next day. She e-mails her professors and keeps up with her work from her missed classes. We still don't really know why she came home, or what's going on with Bean. Every time we ask her what she's thinking, she gives some vague answer that doesn't make much sense.

It's nice to have her around, though.

She drives me to school on Monday morning. "You seem so tense," she says. "I get that things between you and Yamir aren't so great right now. And this Travis kid likes you. So that's not really a bad thing. But what else?"

"Well, that's kind of a lot to have going on all at once, don't you think?" I ask.

"It *is* a lot. But the thing is, people break up, Luce. It's a fact of life." I wonder if she's saying that for me or for herself.

Maybe she's considering breaking up with Bean, because he's making her decide something that's two years away. "You're only in eighth grade. Lots of things are going to change as you get older."

"I know that," I mumble. "But that's not the only thing going on."

"Okay." She parks in front of the school and turns to me. "Well, if that's the case, then you need to tell me the other things. You have to tell people what's happening. People can't help you if you don't fill them in."

Again, I wonder if she's saying that for me or for herself.

I say, "I want to, but it's harder than it seems. I can't always explain how I'm feeling. It's like I'm confused by my own feelings. And if I'm confused, then how can I expect other people to understand?"

She nods. "I know what you mean. I'm always here to listen, though. And you can talk through the confusion. I'll try my best to understand."

"Thank you," I say, as I get out of the car. "For the ride and the advice."

I walk into school, and Erica is already waiting for me at my locker. "We need to talk," she says. "Upstairs bathroom in five minutes."

Sunny's sitting on the floor cramming for a social studies test, and she looks up at me. "She's scary."

I nod. I wonder if that's all Sunny is going to say to me. She never called me back.

"You better go," Sunny tells me after I've hung up my coat and put my books in my locker.

"You want to come?" I ask her.

"No, thanks." She doesn't look up from her social studies book.

I trudge up the stairs to meet Erica and wish that I had someone with me. She's pretty much past her pranks, but what if she gets inspired again and pushes my head into the toilet? I don't think she's ever done that, and I've never heard of that happening outside the movies, but if anyone was going to do it, it would be her.

I walk in and Erica and Zoe are sitting on the counter next to the sinks.

"What's up?" I ask. "Hi, Zoe."

"Hey," she says.

"First of all, cute skirt," Erica says. I look down, because I've already forgotten what I put on this morning. I'm wearing a burgundy corduroy skirt and thick gray tights.

"Thanks."

155

"Second of all," Erica continues, "remember what I said on the phone. I mean it, Lucy. I need this Elias thing to happen. I need you and Yamir to be on good terms."

Zoe jumps in. "But if she's with Yamir, then how can she be with Travis and then help me with Gavin?"

"Zoe, stop," Erica whines. "She already tried to help you. She gave you that whole rap idea. So enough. We'll get to you later."

Zoe stops talking and Erica whispers in my ear, "Don't stress about the Gavin stuff. I'm pretty sure he doesn't like her, so there's no point spending time on it. We'll talk later."

I look at Zoe, and she's staring at her dangling feet. I guess their honeymoon period as friends is over. And I'm pretty sure Zoe heard everything Erica just said. She has a loud whisper.

"Third of all, and most important, the Masquerade is in less than a month. Crunch time. We need to get the makeup schedule figured out; we need to finalize the theme. We need to make sure everyone we care about has a date."

I'm not sure I know who would be included in the "everyone we care about" list, so I ignore that part.

"Okay, let's have a planning meeting," I tell them. "We'll put up some posters telling everyone about the time and place, and whoever wants to come can come."

"No. That's too many people," Erica explains. "Just a small

group: you, me, Zoe, Sunny, and maybe Annabelle, since she's class president."

"Sure. That sounds good."

"Oh, and Evan and the twins," Erica adds. "We need boys too."

"Got it." I ignore the sinking feeling I get when I think about Travis. If I pretend our drama doesn't exist, maybe it will just go away entirely.

"We're the executive committee," Zoe says, clearly repeating something Erica must have told her.

"After school today?" I ask.

"Yeah, school library at 3:45," Erica tells us, hopping down from the sink counter. "You tell Sunny and Annabelle. I'll tell the boys."

We leave the bathroom just before the first bell rings, and I'm suddenly overcome with this feeling of gratitude for Erica. I need a project. I need something to focus on besides the end of my relationship with Yamir.

Maybe I can't make sure Elias likes Erica, or Gavin likes Zoe, or the AGE girls are happy and included, but I can make this Masquerade the best one Old Mill Middle School has ever had.

I hold the key to the best makeup artists and makeup in all of Connecticut.

And everyone knows that makeup is the most important part of a costume. The face is the first thing you see when you're talking to someone. You look into the person's eyes. You notice their smile. Makeup is all about highlighting the face. Sure, you can have cool pants or a cool shirt or even cool shoes. But the makeup makes the costume. The makeup is what everyone will notice and what everyone will remember.

At lunch I tell Annabelle and Sunny about the meeting while Eve and Georgina are in line for the salad bar.

"I have the biggest science test tomorrow," Annabelle says. "I'm super stressed."

"It'll be a quick meeting," I assure her. "You're the class president. You have to be there."

"I know," she groans.

I look at Sunny. She's picking the cucumbers out of her Greek salad. "Will you be there?"

"Yup," is all she says.

Annabelle gets up to find some ketchup, and I turn to Sunny. "Sun, what's with you? You're mad and it's killing me. We need to talk."

"I'm sorry it's killing you," she says. "But what happened at the twins' party was really messed up. You kissed someone else, and then you get my brother and his friends to come for Erica like everything is totally normal."

"That's not what happened!" I yell, feeling stares from Mr. Marblane, the teacher on lunch duty. "That's not what happened," I say again, this time in a whisper.

"Fine. Whatever. Let's talk later."

"Finish your lunch and let's go to the upstairs bathroom."

She rolls her eyes. "Fine."

It's only 11:55 and I'm headed to the upstairs bathroom for my second time today. Everyone knows the upstairs bathroom is the place for secret, important girl meetings, and it's not healthy to have more than one of those in a day.

"See you at the meeting later," Annabelle says as Sunny and I gather up our stuff to leave the table.

I look at Eve and Georgina. Thankfully, they're busy cramming for a test and don't hear us. At least I don't think they do.

I hate leaving people out. In my mind, it's as bad as stealing or physically hurting someone. But this wasn't my choice. It was Erica's. And there wasn't much I could do about it—not when Erica knows I've been lying about Yamir for so long. I'm completely under her thumb.

"Look, Sunny," I start as soon as we're upstairs and no one else is in sight. "I see how you can feel like I'm a total jerk. But that's not the whole story."

"So tell me the whole story," Sunny says.

"First of all, Erica stole my phone and invited Yamir. I had nothing to do with that."

"Uh-huh," Sunny says.

Then I explain the thing about Travis and the planetarium and how I told him it shouldn't have happened. I tell her about how Yamir has been ignoring me for so long now. How he never calls or texts or anything.

"Boyfriends aren't supposed to ignore you," I tell her.

"True."

"And believe me, I'm so upset about this. I mean, Yamir is Yamir. He's a really big deal to me. I know that sounds weird because I'm only thirteen and he's your brother. But I really care about him. I think I'll always care about him."

She gives me a scrunched-up, pained look. "So then why did you even go into that planetarium with Travis?"

"I don't know," I say. "I didn't know how to get out of it. I shouldn't have."

She stays quiet for a little bit. "The thing is, I love you, Luce. But Yamir's my brother, and it seems like you really hurt him."

"He hurt me too. He hurt me first." I glare at her. "Don't you see that?"

She shrugs. "I guess."

"Maybe we shouldn't discuss it," I say reluctantly. I really need a best friend right now, but I don't know how to tell her that. Claudia made such a big deal about being honest with people. "It's weird because he's your brother. I get that. We can't make this an issue between us."

"Fine," she says. "I just heard the bell. We can't be late for class again."

"Right. Let's go."

We leave the upstairs bathroom, and I think we've come to an agreement. I hope so, anyway. And I hope I don't have any more upstairs bathroom meetings for the rest of the week. Maybe even the month.

In between my classes later in the day, Mrs. Deleccio finds me in the hallway.

"So, what's the latest on the composting, Lucy?" she asks. She's carrying a huge stack of science books, and I take some of them to help her.

"Oh, I've been researching, but it's really complicated. We'll need to get approval from the town, figure out where to get the containers and where to put them, and then we'll need to decide who will take care of emptying them," I tell her. "Plus, I'm really worried the kids will be grossed out. It will take time to convince them." I pause. I'm exhausted thinking about it all. "I'm trying, but I've been so busy with homework and Eighth-Grade Masquerade prep."

"Okay, well, you suggested it, and it seems like a good idea, so I hope you can follow through with it." She smiles.

"I will." I walk with her to her classroom to drop off her books. I should just admit that this composting idea is too much for me. I don't know why I haven't acknowledged that yet. Sometimes people take on too much. And that's what I've done.

Maybe it's like Claudia said—you have to talk to people and be honest and tell them how you feel, or they can't help you.

Instead of pretending I can handle it, I just need to be honest and admit that I can't.

Lucy's tip for surviving eighth grade:
Learn how to work with others and be part of a team.

Erica and Zoe are already in the library when I arrive after school. They're sitting in the reading nook under the windows.

"Hey," Zoe says. Erica ignores me.

Soon the twins arrive, and Travis sits down right next to me. "What's up, Desberg?" he asks.

So I guess we're doing the whole last-name thing now. I wasn't even sure he knew my last name.

"Not much. You?" I look up at him and realize he has a group of freckles above his right eyebrow. Gavin doesn't have them. Maybe that's how their mom told them apart when they were little.

"I totally failed that science quiz," he says. "But Mr. Poolis says we can retake it."

"Oh. Cool."

He looks at me like he has more to say but then stays quiet.

Soon everyone else arrives, and Erica goes down her agenda. Mr. Marblane is the faculty adviser for the eighth grade, so he's automatically in charge of overseeing the Masquerade. He mostly stays quiet, though, and lets us do the work.

We discuss the kind of food we should have, the decorations, and the music, and then Erica says, "And Lucy has offered to do everyone's makeup at her family's spa."

"Not for free," I explain. "But I'll give a discount. Twenty dollars a person."

Zoe and Erica look at each other.

"That sounds fair," Zoe says. "My mom gets her makeup done all the time. It's way more than that."

Erica nods and types something into her phone. "Okay, Lucy, put up a sign-up sheet and send an e-mail to everyone in the grade by next week. Make sure you make a list of all the time slots, and allow enough time for everyone."

"I got it," I say.

The meeting ends and Sunny tells me she has to go see the art teacher to discuss the art fair at the end of the year. She doesn't tell me to wait or that her mom will give me a ride home.

"Talk later," is all she says.

"My mom can drive you home," Travis tells me on the way out. "Gavin's going over to Evan's house. So it's just me."

"Oh, okay." I smile. "Thanks."

We walk out together, and he's telling me about this new movie that's coming out. Something about these three teenagers going on a crazy trip to Australia. It sounds really good, the way he's describing it.

We sit outside on the ledge in front of the school. It's February but it feels warmer, like spring is getting ready to start.

I look at Travis and I realize something. He's not Yamir. And I can't expect him to be Yamir. But Yamir disappointed me. And Travis seems okay. Maybe even better than okay.

I want a date for the Masquerade, and I'd be lying if I said that kissing Travis was completely gross. It wasn't. It lasted for half a second, but it was kind of a nice half a second.

Erica will be mad at me for not making up with Yamir, but it's not like I have a choice. I can't make Yamir like me. I can't make Yamir pay attention to me. But I can give Travis a chance.

"Hey, Travis?"

"Yeah?"

"Remember the other night, in your planetarium?"

He nods.

"I'm sorry I pushed you away," I tell him. "I hope you'll give me another chance."

All he says is "Cool," and then he goes back to talking about that movie. Something about how the teenagers are attacked by giant bottles of root beer. It's starting to sound a little dumb, but I don't really mind.

I think this has the potential to be something good.

Travis's mom drops me off, and Mom, Dad, and Grandma are sitting on the front porch. I guess they noticed the warm February temperatures and wanted to take advantage of them too.

"Who was that?" Mom asks.

"Oh, that new kid Travis's mom," I explain and walk inside. I don't want any more questions. "Is Claudia still here?" I ask, from inside the house.

"Until tomorrow morning," Dad says. "I'll take her to the airport on the way to work."

I go upstairs and find Claudia in her room, on her bed, reading some gossip magazine.

I pop my head in. "Hi, Claud."

"Hey. Come sit." She pats the spot next to her and closes the magazine.

I sit with her on her bed. It's like it used to be before she went away to school. "So, listen, I wasn't telling the whole truth," she starts. Shock of the century. I can't wait to hear what the whole truth is.

"Yeah?"

"Bean did ask me to marry him. But in a joking kind of way. He even gave me a Ring Pop."

"Oh. Yum. What flavor?" I smile, even though I know that's not important.

"Strawberry. Duh." She rolls her eyes. "Anyway, then Yamir e-mailed me."

"Huh? What?"

"He told me what happened at that party. And he e-mailed me to ask for advice. I was shocked. It seems so unlike him." She stops talking for a second, I guess to gauge my reaction.

"He asked you to fly home?"

"No. Obviously not." She cracks up. "I got the e-mail after I landed in Connecticut, so it was kind of perfect timing. I wanted to see what Mom and Grandma would say about the Bean thing. And Dad too. And I got to check on you as an added bonus."

"Well, thanks."

"So, can you tell me what's really going on, Luce? The whole story. You've given me little bits and pieces, but I wish you'd tell me everything so I can help."

I shrug. "I guess. But where should I start?"

"At the beginning."

I start talking. I tell her about how Yamir started ignoring me. How I tried to act like I didn't care. I tell her about our middle-of-the-night talk that one night, and how nothing changed. And then about Sienna. And then about Travis and the planetarium. And the kiss.

"Uh-huh," is all she says.

"So what do you think?"

She waits to speak. It seems like she's carefully weighing her options, choosing her words.

"I think you're in eighth grade, and it's okay not to know. It's okay to change your mind."

I nod. That seems a little lame to me. That's it?

"Here's the thing: boys are kind of dumb sometimes. They don't pick up on cues. And that's why you need to talk to them. Speak your mind. Open up when you're not happy with how things are going. It's really the best way to handle any relationship, but especially a boy-girl one."

"Really? Even with Bean?"

"Um, yes, even with Bean. He proposed with a Ring Pop!"

We both crack up laughing, and then we hear Grandma calling us down for dinner.

"Well, what did Yamir want you to do, anyway?" I ask. "I mean, what was the point of him e-mailing you?"

"I guess he wanted some insight into my little sister," she says. "He seemed all confused. Like the whole thing came out of nowhere."

I stand up. "But that's just it. It totally didn't. He's clueless!"

"I know." She wraps her arms around me and squeezes me tight. "You'll take a little break from each other. It'll be okay."

"But what should I do about Travis?"

She gets a text message but ignores it. "Well, what is your gut telling you?"

"I don't know! That's the problem!" I look at her and wait for her to say something, but I think she's waiting for me to talk. "I mean, he's nice. And I think I should give him a chance. But in the back of my head, I'm always thinking about Yamir."

Claudia nods and puts a pillow behind her head. "I know what you mean. I like Bean and everything, but in the back of my mind I know I'm young and there are so many other people to meet."

"Really?" I ask, completely shocked. "You mean you have doubts?"

"Of course. Everyone has doubts!"

"I don't believe you."

"Luce, come on. Of course I do."

"Yeah, but you always seem so confident in your decisions. Maybe some people have doubts, but not you."

Claudia rolls her eyes. "Believe me. I do."

"But, Claud, you're basically the smartest person I know. If you ever have doubts, just call me, and I'll reassure you that you're doing the right thing."

"Thanks, Luce."

I wrap my arms around her and hug her as tight as I possibly can. "I'm really going to miss you, Claud."

She squeezes me back, just as tight. "Me too, Luce. I hope you know how much I love you."

Downstairs, Mom, Dad, and Grandma are all sitting at the table. There's a steaming platter of eggplant Parmesan and an overflowing bowl of spaghetti. Claudia's favorite meal. Plus, there's a wooden bowl of Caesar salad.

"How's everyone?" Dad asks, serving the salad.

Mom launches into another story about Adrienne's crazy animals. At this point we've started tuning her out. Grandma tells us about this lady who seems to come in for a spa treatment every single day. And that's when I realize it's been a long time since I've been at the pharmacy and the spa. I miss it.

"That reminds me, I need to talk to you guys about the spa," I tell them. "Remember when you said it was okay for everyone to get their makeup done there for the Masquerade?"

Mom and Grandma look at each other.

"You said yes," I remind them.

"Okay. We said yes." Grandma puts some eggplant onto Claudia's plate.

"I want to come up with a schedule so we make sure everyone has enough time and gets what they want. And I want to make sure all the staff is working that day."

They assure me that they'll take care of it, but I get nervous they'll forget. "I'll come in tomorrow after school. I want to talk to everyone. We have less than a month, and the spa might already have some bookings."

"Sounds good, Luce." Mom smiles and twirls some spaghetti around her fork.

Later I go to bed, but I can't fall asleep. I keep thinking about Yamir e-mailing Claudia. I want to get up and ask to see the e-mail, but that's probably a bad idea.

In a way I feel better that Yamir does care—in his own weird, Yamir way, at least. But it's also complicated. I already told Travis I wanted to give things with him a chance. And maybe it's too late to fix things with Yamir now anyway.

I toss and turn the whole night. I am going to be so tired tomorrow.

Lucy's tip for surviving eighth grade:
Be nice. Always be nice.

It turns out I don't have much time to think about Yamir or anything else, really, for the next few weeks. I'm too busy getting ready for the Masquerade. At first I was always nervous that Erica was going to turn on me and tell everyone how I basically lied about Yamir. Plus, I was worried she was going to tell Travis terrible things about me. But then one day I realize that she can't. That she won't. She needs me to help plan the Masquerade. She needs me to get the spa ready and have all the staff prepared. She needs me to give the amazing discount.

Sometimes all you really need is to be needed.

"How are things with Elias?" I ask Erica after lunch.

"Amazing, actually." She smiles. I doubt they're really that amazing. But Erica only has two answers to how things are going—amazing or terrible. "We've been hanging out a ton."

"Oh, that's so great."

"Yeah, he'll be at the Masquerade." She smiles. "I guess I'll be the only one with a high school date."

"I guess so." Even though she needs me, she still finds a way to push my buttons.

"But Zoe's so glad you're with Travis. Apparently Gavin was always kind of weird with girls, but now that Travis has a girlfriend, he felt he should step up his game."

"Oh yeah?" I ask.

"I guess. He's still a little weird, though."

The truth is, I haven't hung out with Travis that much. We text at night sometimes, and chat in school, and we've gone for ice cream a few times. That's pretty much it—and that's okay. It may sound heartless, but I don't think about him that much when I'm not with him.

"I gotta get to class," I tell Erica. "So meet me after school and we'll go over to the spa together."

"Got it."

Sunny's already seated when I get to science. "Are you coming to the spa after school?" I ask her. "Erica wants to finalize everything with the spa director."

"Sure."

Things have been fine with us, but not amazing. Not our usual friendship by any means.

"Look, I'm sorry about what happened," I say, even though I still don't think it's my fault. "I think Yamir and I are both to blame. I didn't mean to hurt his feelings, but my feelings were hurt for a long time."

"Yeah. You're right." She turns to look at me, and it seems like it's the first time she understands what I'm saying. Like we may have had a breakthrough.

"I guess I just wanted you and Yamir to go to the dance together, and Evan and me to go together. And I know it's bizarre, because he's my brother and you're my best friend. But it just seems like the four of us should go together. The Masquerade is our last hurrah."

"Yeah. I know what you mean. I was so obsessed with making this last semester of middle school perfect. It was, like, the most important thing ever." I move my desk closer to hers. "But it's so not our last hurrah. It's just the beginning."

"You think?"

I nod.

"What if everything changes when we get to high school?" Sunny asks me. "It's so big, and we may not have classes together. And Evan can meet other girls. And Yamir could fail out!"

I burst out laughing when she says that. It's kind of funny but also kind of sad. Yamir doesn't work so hard in school. He always does well anyway, but that could change.

"But seriously, what if we don't get to have lunch together anymore?" Sunny asks.

"I won't be able to play 'guess the spice' anymore, then!"

Sunny frowns. "But it's our favorite game!"

Sunny and I started this thing where I guess the spices that are in her Indian-cuisine lunches. I've gotten pretty good, and I've learned so many new spices.

"Sun, some things may change, but not everything," I tell her.

"How do you know?"

"I just know. We'll always be BFFs. No matter what. We've made it this long. I mean, things changed when we went from Old Mill Elementary to Old Mill Middle. And we stayed BFFs through it all."

"True." Sunny puts her head down on the desk. "You promise?"

"I promise."

Soon Mrs. Diver comes in and it's time for class. Sunny picks her head up, and I smile at her and she smiles at me. Knowing smiles. Smiles that mean everything will be okay.

Sunny and I are back.

Sunny's mom drives us over to the spa and she's nice to me, the way she always is. I was a little bit worried she'd be upset or mad about Yamir. Sunny sits in front, and Erica and I sit in back.

Soon we're at the spa. Mom, Grandma, and Penelope, the manager, are waiting for us in the reception area. I wonder if Mom and Grandma had to warn Penelope about Erica.

"Lucy!" Penelope stands up and hugs me. "And you must be Sunny and Erica?"

It feels funny that Penelope doesn't know who Sunny is. Sunny used to know all the pharmacy employees, because we used to be together at the store all the time. I guess we're busier now. Maybe that's why Sunny's so worried about things changing once we're in high school. Things have already started changing.

"Follow me, girls. Can I get you anything?" Penelope asks.

"I'd love some of this fruit water," Erica says. "How fancy!"

"Of course."

When we first started planning the spa, I knew we had to have water with fruit. It's the most elegant, delicious drink. Today there's a pitcher of water with apple pieces and orange pieces. We all fill up tall glasses and follow Penelope to her office.

A seat is set up for each of us with a special Pink & Green spa pad and our signature pink pens.

This feels very official. I wonder if Mom and Grandma

told Penelope to take this seriously, or if she knew to do it on her own.

"So I've already blocked off the whole day of the Masquerade. All our cosmetologists will be working, and we won't be booking any other appointments," Penelope says. "I just need to know what time the event starts, so we know when to schedule the appointments."

I look at Erica.

"It starts at seven in the evening." Erica sounds so formal that it's hard for me to keep a straight face.

"Okay, and how many people will be getting their makeup done?" Penelope asks.

"Well, people are still signing up," Erica explains. "We should have that by the end of the week. We'd like the whole grade to come in, but we obviously can't force them."

Penelope smiles. "Right."

"There are ninety-seven kids in the grade," Erica says.

"Well, we have six treatment rooms," Penelope says. "And we can always make room for people to get makeup done in the reception area if need be. We'll make it work."

I start to get nervous. Imagine if everyone wants their makeup done. And then what if people show up late and mess up the whole schedule? If Grandma's around, she'll get super stressed. There will be yelling.

This suddenly seems like a lot to take on.

"Thanks so much," Erica says.

"No problem." Penelope looks at Sunny and me. "Do you have any questions?"

Sunny shakes her head. "I don't think so," I say.

"Don't worry, Lucy," Penelope says, smiling. "It's going to be perfect."

I guess Penelope could read my mind. Or my facial expression.

Lucy's tip for surviving eighth grade:
Go with your gut feeling.

I get home and there's an e-mail from Travis:

Yo LD.
Are we coordinating costumes for the Masquerade?
What's the deal? Wanna come over tomorrow after
school?
—T

Wow. I hadn't even thought about coordinating costumes. I don't know if I want to coordinate with Travis. The thought of it seems cheesy and potentially awkward. I don't know him well enough to do that.

Maybe it was easier the way Yamir's class did it last year. No dates. They all agreed on that, and everyone was cool with it. Now there's all this pressure. Will Sunny and Evan wear matching outfits? Will Zoe and Gavin? I really don't know.

And what about the AGE girls? The Masquerade is getting close and they still don't have dates.

So much to worry about. So little time.

I call Sunny with a new plan. I need her to go along with it. She probably will. But Erica's an issue. I have a feeling she's going to hate this idea.

I don't know what I'm thinking, but I call Sunny's house phone instead of her cell phone.

And Yamir answers. He obviously knows it's me, because they have caller ID. I can't hang up. I have to talk. I don't have a choice.

"Hey, Yamir. Is Sunny there?"

"Yeah. Hold on."

I guess I didn't expect much more than that when I heard Yamir's voice on the other end of the phone. Or maybe I did. I really don't know.

"What's up?" Sunny asks. She sounds all out of breath.

"Are you okay? What's wrong?" I ask her.

"I'm fine." She laughs. "I was trying on clothes. It's a major workout for me!"

It's true. Sunny's closet is pretty big, and she has to dig all the way to the back to find some stuff.

"So, Travis e-mailed me to ask about coordinating costumes for the Masquerade, and it got me thinking," I tell her. "I want to veto dates. There's no way everyone's going to have a date. And it's not fair."

"That's kind of crazy, Luce. You can't tell people what to do."

"But people can still dance together," I say. "The thing is, it doesn't need to be, like, a major date event. If people pair off, that's okay, but they don't have to make a big deal ahead of time."

"I don't know. I think people are gonna be disappointed."

"You mean you think Erica is going to be disappointed?"

"Well, yeah."

We go back and forth with this, and the more we talk, the more I realize how urgent this is. There's no way I can guarantee that everyone in the grade has a date. But there's no reason for people to be miserable either.

We have to find a way to make going without dates seem cooler and more fun.

There has to be a way. I just have to figure out what it is.

I've had so many missions this year: completing the green cafeteria work, making sure this was the perfect last semester, doing all that I could to make the AGE girls feel included and happy, helping Zoe with Gavin, even helping Erica with Elias. Maybe it shows a lack of focus to change missions so many times. The thing is, it takes time to find the right one.

It takes time to realize which one is most important. But at least I discovered it before it was too late.

I don't want anyone to have negative feelings about our Masquerade.

I hang up with Sunny and realize that I need to have a meeting with Erica and Zoe right away. I know what it'll take to convince them: it needs to seem official, secretive, and exclusive.

I call the spa and Penelope answers.

"Hi, Lucy!" Penelope says when she realizes it's me. "Getting excited for your event?"

"We need to have another meeting at the spa," I tell her. "It needs to feel fancy and important."

"I can do that, of course—but what's this all about?"

"I don't think it's fair if some people have dates and some don't, and there's no way everyone who wants to have a date will have one. So I want to convince Erica and Zoe, who are basically in charge of everything, that we should encourage everyone to go with their friends. No official dates."

"I see," Penelope says.

"But if we tell them at the spa, with fancy lemonade and tea sandwiches and make Erica feel really important, there's more of a chance that she'll go along with it."

"Okay." Penelope pauses, and I hear typing in the background. "I know just what to do."

At lunch the next day, the AGE girls are obsessing about not having dates, and I know I've made the right decision.

"Dates aren't that big of a deal," I say, just to see what Erica's reaction will be. I'm not sure when it started, but Erica and Zoe sit at our table every day now. If you had asked me in fifth grade if Erica Crane and I would ever share a lunch table, I would have said absolutely not. But here we are.

"Lucy, yes they are!" Erica says. "I mean, if you don't have one, you're not going to die or anything, but it's better to have a date."

I respond, "I'm not sure about that."

Erica glares at me after that, and I go back to my turkey sandwich. I don't want to get into a huge argument about it. Not yet.

"Guys," Erica leans in to the table and tries to get everyone's attention. "Lucy's just bitter because she and Yamir broke up."

"Erica!" I exclaim. She's going to say more. She's going to say I lied to impress them, and that Yamir was never really my boyfriend. Everything she's threatened to do.

She stops talking, but I worry there's more to come.

"So you're still going through with this plan," Sunny whispers to me as we leave lunch.

"I am. I mean, did you see how the AGE girls seemed today? They're all worked up about it. It's not fair. And it's not only them."

"I think you're right," Sunny says. "But I don't know if it will work out. That's all I'm saying. You can't save the whole world, you know."

"You'll get the e-mail after school. Penelope is making it look all nice and fancy. Just wait."

"Whatever you say, Lucy." Sunny rolls her eyes at me. "And by the way, Yamir keeps asking me if you have a date. Just figured I'd let you know that."

"He does?" My heart flips over like a pancake.

"Yup."

As happy as that makes me, I have to push it out of my head. I told Travis I'd give him a chance. I want to give him a chance. And I'm trying to veto dates anyway. What difference does it make that Yamir wants to know? He didn't behave like a boyfriend, so he can't be my boyfriend. That's just the way it is.

Lucy's tip for surviving eighth grade:
Sometimes fancy is better.

𝒜s soon as ℰrica gets the e-mail, she sends me a text:

Fanciest e-mail I've ever gotten. Z & I will be there.

I knew it would work. Erica can't resist fancy stuff. Penelope set it up to look like an invitation to a black-tie party. And she mentioned the artisan finger sandwiches and sparkling lemonade we'll be having.

When Penelope tells her that it's actually much more sophisticated to go with your friends and not be paired up, Erica will totally believe it. Penelope used to live in Manhattan, and she wears fancy shoes. She's pretty much Erica's idol.

I'm over at Travis's house, and we're playing some video

game where you need to squash all these killer tomatoes. It's pretty tame as far as video games go, but I'm not really feeling it.

"So, what did you decide about the costume?" Travis asks me, taking a sugar cookie off the platter his mom set up for us.

"I don't think we should go all matchy-matchy," I say, putting down the controller. He beat me three games in a row. "It's just a little cheesy. And not everyone's gonna match with someone. So let's just do our own thing."

He puts his feet up on the ottoman. The bottom of his socks are almost black, even though he has the cleanest house I've ever seen. "Okay, cool."

I can't tell if he really cares. Ever since I said I'd give things a chance, he doesn't seem to care as much about me. I wonder if that's how life works. You try so hard to get someone to like you. And then when they do like you, you don't really care anymore. It's kind of depressing.

"I'm gonna go shoot hoops. Wanna come?"

Maybe I should remind him that it's February in Connecticut and it's freezing outside. Truthfully I don't care if he goes to play basketball, but I don't want to sit in the freezing cold.

"It's kind of cold out, isn't it?" I ask.

"Yeah, I guess so." He looks at me and shrugs. "Well, we'll bundle up."

So Travis puts on a hooded sweatshirt and his coat, and I put my coat on too, and we go out front, and he shoots hoops and I sit on the wooden rocking chair on his front porch.

I'm not sure if I've ever been so bored or so freezing in my whole life. I'm not sure it's possible for Travis's personality to change so drastically so fast, but something seems wrong. Maybe he's bored with me. Or he can tell that I'm bored with him.

I text Sunny that I'm at his house and bored, and we start texting back and forth about other random stuff. I feel guilty about this, but the whole time I'm sitting here, I keep wishing that I was watching Yamir shoot hoops instead of Travis. And I keep wishing that Sunny would mention something else about Yamir. It's terrible.

But she doesn't. Travis keeps playing until I say, "I think I have to go. It's getting kinda late."

He shoots the ball another time, and when it bounces off the backboard and rolls away, he doesn't rush to get it.

"Oh, okay. Cool."

He comes over to me and puts his hand on my shoulder. "I had some good shots, didn't I?"

"Yeah." I force a smile. "Definitely."

We go back inside, and I wait for Grandma to pick me up. Gavin's on the couch in the den, watching some sports show and throwing popcorn into his mouth. Their mom is in the kitchen, stirring something on the stove.

The longer I stay here, the more I get the feeling that Travis and I just don't have a lot to say to each other. We have pretty much nothing in common, I guess. And that makes our time together really boring. Almost in a painful way. Yamir may be thoughtless, but our time together is never boring.

Finally Grandma comes and I say good-bye, and yell out, "Bye, Mrs. Landes." She turns away from the stove and waves but doesn't say anything. She's cold and a little sad looking. I guess she really misses Chicago.

"Did you have a nice time?" Grandma asks me as soon as my seat belt is buckled.

I nod. "Yeah, I guess."

"You guess?"

I shrug and try to figure out how to explain. I don't know what it is, but I get the feeling that Grandma will have an interesting perspective on this.

"Do you think polite people can just be really boring when you get to know them?" I ask.

"Perhaps. It's still good to be polite, though."

"I know." I change the radio station to something quieter. It's a little strange that Grandma was listening to such loud music. "It's just . . . I think Travis is kind of boring. He seemed all nice and sensitive and stuff at first. And now he's sort of just a regular boy. Nothing special."

"I see," Grandma says, looking at me for a second and then back at the road in front of her. "Well, that's why you're not marrying these boys. You have time to find someone who's just the right amount of boring."

"You mean everyone's boring?" My face crumples. What a depressing thought.

"In their own way. You'll see. It's not always a bad thing."

I usually believe Grandma, since she's old and wise and she's been through so much. But right now I don't want to believe her. I *can't* believe her. Yamir's not boring, and maybe in eighth grade that's really all that matters.

29

Lucy's tip for surviving eighth grade:
Do for others.

All throughout school the next day, Erica keeps bringing up the fancy meeting. That's what she calls it. "I can't wait for the fancy meeting, Lucy," she says after math. "Penelope is so cool to schedule such a fancy meeting," she says before lunch.

I keep shushing her, because I don't want the AGE girls to hear and feel left out. I mean, they haven't been that involved in the planning for the Masquerade, but still. It's not nice to keep talking about something in front of other people when you know they're not included. It's purposefully mean, even.

"Okay, okay, Lucy." She rolls her eyes at me. "Calm down."

She should not be telling me to calm down, when we're talking about my meeting and she's the one who's overexcited, but I let it go. I need her on my side. Meanwhile, the AGE girls are still stressing about the date situation. Eve thinks she's going to bring this boy from Madison who went to camp with her, and I tell her that's crazy. It's not that big of a deal to have a date.

"Not everyone feels that way," she tells me over and over again.

Mrs. Deleccio finds me after lunch, even though I've been trying to avoid her.

"I'm so sorry. I dropped the ball on the composting," I admit. "I've just been so busy."

"It's okay, Lucy." She smiles like it really is okay, but I still feel guilty. I tell her I'm going to try to work on it. Maybe after the Masquerade is over.

"We appreciate all your hard work," she says, and gently pats my arm.

I should never have suggested it.

Finally the end of the day rolls around, and it's almost time for our meeting. Sunny and I get there first. Penelope has rearranged her whole office so there's a table for food and another table for drinks and a small circle of chairs to the side.

"How does it look?" she asks us.

"Perfect," I tell her.

There are finger sandwiches, fruit kabobs, and mini quiches on the food table. The drinks table is overflowing with mini bottles of sparkling water, a pitcher of bubbly pink lemonade, and a fancy water jug with strawberries and pineapple in it.

Erica and Zoe arrive a few minutes later. Erica's wearing a chunky gray sweater dress with red tights and shiny black ballet flats. She looks like she's going to the opera. Zoe's just wearing jeans, but her fancy designer ones with a tiny little hole above the right knee. And she has on a cream cashmere sweater that hits at the perfect spot on her hips.

"You guys look great," Penelope says. "Please get some food and drink and come sit."

"This is like a wedding!" Erica exclaims. "Mini quiche? Amazing!"

I wink at Penelope, even though I'm not so good at winking.

"So, ladies, we're getting very excited about the big event. I've discussed it with Doris and Jane, and we'd love to offer all the students a special Pink and Green goody bag after their makeup appointment. We'll put in some lotions and cleansers, maybe a special aromatherapy candle?"

"That's incredible," Zoe squeals. "Everyone is going to flip!"

I see what Penelope's doing—buttering them up. And it's working!

"And have you considered a theme for the dance?" Penelope asks. "I was the president of my sorority in college, so believe me, I've planned many, many dances in my day. The theme is always key."

Zoe and Erica look at each other, and then they look at Sunny and me. We're all sitting here staring at one another. It's actually kind of funny.

"Maybe something low-key but cool. Since we live near the ocean, what about 'Under the Sea'?" I suggest.

"Yeah, that's cool, but kind of overdone," Erica says.

"Or maybe black-and-white movies," Zoe suggests. "Like, we can have each table be an old movie, and then everyone can wear black or white."

Sunny jumps in. "Well, don't forget that people are going to come in costumes. So the theme is the Masquerade. We already have a theme, kind of."

"True, true." Penelope nods. I wonder if she really cares about the theme, or if she's just trying to get everyone talking and then she's going to bring up the date thing.

"Well, here's an idea," Erica says, and I immediately get scared. My heart pounds every time that girl is about to speak—Erica's ideas tend to be dangerous. "Since Pink and Green is doing so much to make this event awesome, what if the theme were a little bit about Pink and Green?"

We all stare at Erica as she talks. Penelope's sitting back in her rolling chair all calm and collected, almost like she knew something like this would happen. Sunny's mouth is hanging open. I know exactly how she feels.

"Go on," Penelope says, scribbling some notes in her Pink & Green spiral notebook.

Erica smiles, seeming pleased that she has the floor. "It wouldn't be anything too crazy. Just a little bit of Pink and Green branding. Like, people need to wear pink or green, or incorporate it into their costumes."

"Yeah," Sunny jumps in again. "And we can take the green to the next level: the dance should be environmentally friendly. The cafeteria and pretty much the whole school are green. So the dance has to be too!"

"Oh, totally," Zoe says, clearly feeling like she has to say something.

"I got it." Erica leans back in her chair. "You ready?"

We all nod. Penelope takes a sip of her sparkling water. This level of suspense should probably be reserved for a presidential election.

Erica takes a deep breath. "Eighth-Grade Masquerade: Pink and Green Is the New Black."

"Oh my goodness," I shout. "That is unbelievable!"

"Unbelievable good or unbelievable bad?" Erica asks, and I swear that's the first time I've ever seen her be uncertain.

"Unbelievable good," I say. I don't say that it's even more unbelievable because Erica's the one saying it, and that Erica's the one bringing up the branding thing in the first place.

"Do you get it?" Erica asks. "Because, like, people always wear black to fancy events. And we're shaking things up!"

"Wonderful! I love what's happening here," Penelope tells us. "This event is going to be amazing in every way."

Soon everyone is silent, like there isn't anything else to talk about. I start to get worried. Did Penelope forget the purpose of the meeting?

"I have to say one more thing," Penelope says. "And I know it's going to seem a little out of left field. But from my experience, these events work better when everyone goes as friends."

Zoe cocks her head at Penelope. "We're all friends."

"I mean, no dates. It turns people away if they feel like they have to find a partner." She pauses and takes a bite of her finger sandwich. "Think about it this way: you want as many people to come as possible, right?"

We nod.

"Well, I'm sure there are kids who won't have dates, and they'll just decide to stay home," Penelope continues. "And you guys want 100 percent attendance. I mean, of course there's going to be someone sick or someone out of town or someone with family plans. But you want to aim for 100 percent."

"But we want dates," Erica whines. "We want it to feel like a mature event."

"I know," Penelope says. "But mature with low attendance or a little less mature with high attendance?" She pauses. "Think about it."

"I don't know," Zoe says. "I mean, Gavin and I are really excited about going together. It's kind of a big deal for us."

Penelope nods, tight-lipped.

"And what about Elias?" Erica says. "I mean, I have a high school boyfriend. If we don't have dates, why would he even come? He won't. And then this whole thing will have been pointless."

"What whole thing?" Sunny asks, genuinely confused. "You're having fun together, right? You have a boyfriend who's in high school. That's cool."

"Not enough." Erica folds her arms across her chest. "I want dates to the dance. And I'm in charge of this event. No one else wanted to do it, so I am in charge."

I look at Sunny and she looks at me. Penelope studies Erica carefully but doesn't say anything.

I don't know what to say.

"This is just because Yamir doesn't like you anymore,"

Erica says to me, and it stings worse than anything she's said in the past. "So since you don't have a date, you don't want anyone to have a date."

I mutter, "That's not true," but then I start to wonder: what if it is? I don't think it is. But maybe some deep-down part of me does feel that way.

"It *is* true." Erica shoots eye daggers at me.

"It isn't, because I have Travis, remember?" I raise my eyebrows at her. "He could be my date if I wanted one."

"You don't like him. Everyone knows it. Probably even Travis."

So now Erica and I are having this battle in front of Zoe, Sunny, and Penelope, and I don't know what to do.

"Erica, please," I say. "Look, I know this is a change, but at least give it some thought. Take a few days to think about it. And consider everyone else in the grade. We want them to have good memories of their Eighth-Grade Masquerade."

"Fine. I'll give it some thought," she says, mocking me. She looks down at her plate. "I'm going to have another mini quiche."

Soon Zoe's mom comes to pick up her and Erica, and Sunny and I stay for a few more minutes to talk to Penelope.

"Well, it was worth a shot," Penelope says.

"Yeah, I guess."

"It's going to be wonderful no matter what. I promise."
She puts a hand on my shoulder. "And listen, what you're trying to do is really sweet, but you can't always control everything. Some people will have dates and some people won't.
It's the way life works. And you can't make everyone happy all
the time."

"I know." I manage to squeak out a smile. "Thanks for
everything."

Sunny and I walk to the back office to meet my mom,
who's going to drive us home. It feels like a million years ago
that I sat in here and opened the mail and stressed about the
pharmacy staying in business.

I guess old worries just make way for new worries. And
there's not much you can do about that.

30

Lucy's tip for surviving eighth grade:
Admit when you've taken on too much.

*E*rica doesn't talk to me for a whole week. She still sits at our lunch table, but we don't speak. Zoe smiles at me, but that's it. I think they feel like I was trying to ruin their lives or something. Like I was trying to convince them to become nuns. It's a little over the top.

But that's not the worst part. I had a meeting with Mrs. Deleccio about the composting project, and I had to tell her I totally failed and couldn't take it on anymore. I was in over my head trying to sort out all the information, and I couldn't find time to do it. Between homework, planning for the Masquerade, and trying to sleep at night—not to mention worrying about Yamir and Travis (and I didn't mention *that* to her!)—I just couldn't handle anything else.

It felt awful to admit it, knowing I was letting her down. She seemed disappointed. And that's the opposite of how

I wanted to end my time at Old Mill Middle School, with teachers disappointed in me and projects left undone.

And as if that wasn't bad enough, while I was meeting with Mrs. Deleccio, Erica spilled the beans. I wasn't there, so I don't know exactly what happened. But Sunny was there. And she told me.

Apparently it went something like this:

Erica told everyone that I had lied about Yamir, that things hadn't been good for a while, that he didn't want to be with me, and that we had basically broken up. And then she told everyone at the table that I don't even like Travis, but I'm just desperate to have someone, so I'm leading him on.

And now the AGE girls just stare at me all awkward when they see me. Like my cat was run over and they don't know what to say. I tell myself that only our table knows all of this—but that's probably not true. The whole grade probably knows by now.

Sunny hasn't mentioned the Yamir thing in a long time, and it almost seems like she's forgotten about it. I want to ask her about it, because I still think about him way too much.

I don't bring it up, though. Maybe Sunny doesn't want to talk about it. Maybe he really is with that Sienna girl now, and Sunny doesn't want to tell me.

Who knows.

One thing is for sure: I want to end things with Travis. Dates or no dates for the Masquerade, he's not for me. I know that now. I gave him a chance. And we kissed a few times. And we hung out a bunch one-on-one: the movies, after school at his house, even a night trip to the beach. Grandma would have never allowed it, but I didn't tell her. And it was dark and kind of cold, and he brought a blanket. And it seemed like it would be so romantic and amazing—the kind of night I thought I'd remember forever. But then when we got there, it was just so boring. There was nothing to talk about. I tried and tried, but every topic felt stale. And I kept thinking about how much more amazing the night would have been if I had been there with Yamir.

The Masquerade is in a little less than two weeks, and there's still so much to do. But since Erica's not talking to me, I don't get to do any of it. The spa staff handles all the makeover appointments, Erica and Zoe are dealing with decorations, and Annabelle and Sunny are making posters advertising our theme.

I'm at my locker putting books away after school when Travis comes up behind me and wraps his arms around my shoulders, all boyfriendy.

So I guess he hasn't heard Erica's little tirade. Maybe she really only told our table. At least that's something.

"Oh, hi!" I try to sound cheery, but really I'm annoyed. His arms around my shoulders is way too much PDA for me. Maybe things were different in his old school, but here people don't hang on each other much in the halls.

"You want to come over after school? It's such a gloomy day. We can hang in the planetarium?"

"Oh, that sounds like fun, but I can't," I tell him. "I have to study for that social studies test. I've barely even looked at my notes."

"We have a whole week to study," he reminds me. "Come on. It'll be so cozy. I'll make popcorn. We'll turn the sound effects really loud."

"I'm sorry, Travis. I really can't."

"My mom won't be home . . ." He lets his voice trail off, and then I'm even more annoyed. I don't know how Travis started out as the nicest boy in the world and then turned into this.

"Yeah. I'm sorry, Travis." I turn away from him. "I have to go."

That night, I call Sunny and tell her everything. It's late and I'm under the covers and I'm not supposed to be on the phone, but I feel trapped in my thoughts. I need to talk with Sunny.

"Have you been feeling like this for a while?" she asks.

"Yeah," I say. "And I didn't know if I could talk to you. You've been busy with the Masquerade and with Evan. And anyway, I think you're still mad at me."

"Huh? Why?"

"About Yamir," I say softly. Thoughts of Yamir eat away at me like mosquitoes on a hot summer night.

"Oh, Luce. Come on. It was a thing and now it's not a thing. And you're my best friend. I forgot about it."

I don't know if that's good or bad. If she forgot about it, it means it's really over. Too over to ever be a thing again, probably. Like when people try to bring up private jokes from elementary school that no one even remembers anymore.

"Well, I'm glad you're not mad," I say.

"So you never liked Travis?" she asks, changing the topic slightly.

"I mean, I wanted to give him a chance." I flip over onto my back. "And then I might have liked him for a day. He really tries, and it's sweet. But coming from him, it also weirds me out."

Sunny never tells me romantic stuff about Evan. I know they've kissed, and that's it. She never goes into detail about it. She's private, and I don't push her.

"Maybe he's changed since he first moved here," Sunny says. "Or maybe you have."

"Maybe."

Grandma knocks on my door. "Lucy, it's nearly eleven. Off the phone."

"Okay," I yell through the door.

"I gotta go in a sec," I whisper. "Anyway, I need to break up with him. Is that mean, since the dance is so soon?"

"Is being nice your main concern? Or is being honest your main concern?"

I wait for a second to reply. "That's a good question."

"And it looks like people are going to have dates for the dance. So do you want to go without a date?" Sunny asks.

"You're asking such hard questions!" I laugh, but really I want to cry. I don't know how things became so complicated and scary.

"Just think about it," she says. "That's all. Anyway, I gotta go too."

"Bye, Sun. See you tomorrow."

I lie awake most of the night. I don't want to be with Travis. I don't want to go to the dance with him. But I also feel like it's cruel to leave him without a date. But maybe he'd find someone else. I toss and turn all night long. As the minutes tick by, I get more and more nervous.

31

Lucy's tip for surviving eighth grade:
Don't dwell on the negative. Figure out a way to fix it.

I'm still sitting at my kitchen table eating my Honey Nut Cheerios with cut-up banana when my phone buzzes.

It's a text from Erica:

Need to talk to you. Go to second floor bathroom as soon as you get to school.

A part of me thinks maybe she's turning a corner and things are looking up. I only slept for an hour last night, but I feel energized. Things are going to work out. I know it. Sometimes positive thinking is enough to turn everything around. I just need to remember that.

Dad picks me up and drives me to school, and I'm grateful for the time with him. Ten minutes here and ten minutes there are worth so much more than a weeklong visit a few times a year.

We don't even talk much, but he always finds just the right music for a morning drive. Today it's this new Bob Dylan album. And when we do talk, it's quiet and relaxed. He's one of those people who makes me feel calmer just by being around him.

I walk into school and go straight to the second-floor bathroom. I didn't have a chance to text Sunny, and I wonder if Erica sent her the same text.

Or maybe Erica wants it to be a private meeting.

My heart is pounding. I don't want to see Travis on the way there. I can't see him until I know exactly what I plan to say.

Erica's in the bathroom, sitting on the sink counter. Her eyes are red and her skin is blotchy. Tears dot her cheeks.

"Hi," I say, softly. "Are you okay?"

"Do I look okay, Lucy?" She sneers. "Come on. Wake up."

"Sorry," I mumble. "What's wrong?"

"Elias broke up with me. He needs to focus on his work. That's what his mom said, or so he claims."

"His work?"

"Yeah, like schoolwork. I think he's doing really bad in school." She rolls her eyes. "His mom is a crazy person. Like, seriously. He wasn't allowed to watch TV until he was, like, ten."

"Oh." I look down at my boots. They're covered in mud, and I hadn't even realized it. I must be really out of it. I have no idea what his TV allowance has to do with Elias breaking up with her. Maybe it's just easier for Erica to blame his crazy mom.

"Anyway," she says, "I'll do what you want. No dates. If I can't have a date, then no one can have a date."

"Really?" I perk up but try to hide my happiness. It's for a bad reason, but I'm getting my way, and everyone will benefit from Erica's misery. It's kind of perfect, when you think about it.

"Yeah. I'm not going to be the loser without a date," she reminds me. "Zoe's fine with it. She can still do whatever she wants with Gavin, obviously. But I will make sure that no one comes with a date if I don't have one."

It's weird that Zoe's not here. I haven't seen them apart in months. I wonder if Zoe knows about Erica's change of heart yet, or if Erica is telling me first. Maybe she's just saying Zoe is fine with it, but Zoe doesn't even know yet. I wouldn't put it past Erica.

"I'm sorry about Elias," I say. I'm tempted to reach over and give Erica a hug, but I don't think we're there yet. She's still Erica Crane, even if she does sit at our lunch table. And she's never apologized for all the mean things she's said. I think Evan's right about her: she'll probably never be nice.

"Don't tell anyone," she says. "I'm just gonna say you didn't want dates and the executive committee decided."

"Okay."

"I don't need everyone to know he broke up with me." She starts sniffling again. "And if I find out you told anyone, I will completely ruin your life."

Well, I believe *that*. "Your secret is safe with me."

We hear the bell ring and it's time for first period. I silently thank God for making Elias break up with Erica, even though I feel a little bit bad that she's had her heart broken. I know people have free will and everything, but the timing of this is just too perfect. I don't really have to worry about breaking up with Travis now. No dates means no dates for anyone. Perfect. It's divine intervention.

"Where were you this morning?" Sunny asks me as soon as I walk into first period.

"Long story," I whisper.

Mrs. O'Rourke is at the front of the class, writing on the dry-erase board. I know she's going to turn around any second and glare at me for talking.

Sunny says through her teeth, "Tell me."

"Later."

Sunny's annoyed, but there's nothing I can do about it. Zoe is in this class, and she'll overhear me. Plus, Erica swore me to secrecy.

I mean, okay, I will probably tell Sunny, because that doesn't count—we don't keep secrets from each other. And she'll know not to tell anyone. The whole "I won't tell anyone" promise doesn't apply to best friends.

When class ends, Sunny and I walk out together. I need to find a private spot to tell her the big news. Obviously the second-floor bathroom won't work. I have a feeling Erica will be spending a lot of time there today.

"Come with me," I tell Sunny. I lead her down the hall, past the science classrooms, through the library, past the cafeteria, and into the band room.

"What's going on?" she asks. "You're acting crazy. And we're going to be late for English."

"Just *shh.*"

We walk into the big closet where all the instruments are stored. I know there's no band or orchestra class next period, so I think we're safe. At least for a few minutes.

"Elias broke up with Erica," I tell her.

"What? Is that why you seem so happy?" Sunny raises her eyebrows. "I can't believe it. You're meaner than I thought."

"Well, obviously I'm sad for her, but do you know what she said?"

Sunny shakes her head.

"She said we can't have dates at the Masquerade now. She can't be the loser without the date. So it's for the best. Now no one has to suffer."

"Oh no." Sunny holds her head. "I think this is a bigger mess than we realized."

"What do you mean?"

She lets out a huge sigh.

"Okay, so I was telling my parents about the whole no-dates thing over dinner the other night, because you know how they're always saying we're growing up too fast and we should just focus on our studies and stuff?"

"Yeah."

"So I thought they'd be excited that there's a chance we may all go as friends and just hang out, and it wouldn't be a big deal. I told them how you don't want anyone to feel bad. You know how they're obsessed with kindness?" She laughs a little. "But Yamir was there too, and he was pretty quiet, texting someone under the table, the way he normally does." She pauses to roll her eyes. "But maybe he was listening? And he knew it was your idea. And I told them how Erica was basically vetoing it because of Elias."

She stares at me. I'm finally getting the connection here. Or maybe I'm not. Maybe I'm jumping to conclusions because I want Yamir to be thinking about me. It seems like my brain always finds a way to do that.

"Do you think Elias even liked Erica?" I ask her.

"No idea. I mean, did they ever really hang out? It seems like Erica is all talk."

"There's only one person who would know." I pause. "I mean, one person we'd be able to get the information from."

Sunny sighs. "I'll see what I can do."

We leave the instrument closet and head to English.

Erica is brokenhearted, yet this is the happiest I've been in days. Either that makes me a totally evil person or it means I see the silver lining in all bad situations.

Or maybe it's both.

32

Lucy's tip for surviving eighth grade:
Be happy for other people's happiness.

"So? Anything?" I ask Sunny over the phone.

"Nope. He was, like, 'Why would I care about your dumb dance?' and then he walked away."

I huff. "Well, that's rude."

"Yeah. But in the end, who cares? We got what we wanted. Well, what you wanted."

"How did the AGE girls seem at lunch?" I ask. I was finishing math homework at the time. But my mind was all over the place with this Elias thing and the whole Travis situation, so I wasn't sure I was getting anything right.

"They were thrilled. Like, beyond. They're all into their costumes again, and the makeup. And they feel like they can ask anyone to dance, since no one's going to be paired off. Honestly, Luce, you totally made their year."

"Good. That's all I care about." That's a little bit of a lie, since I also care about Yamir. Hopelessly, pathetically, insanely care about Yamir. But Sunny knows that. I don't need to hit her over the head with it.

"Listen, I gotta go finish the science lab. But what about Travis?" Sunny asks.

"My life is kind of made, since there aren't any dates anyway. Do I even need to break up with him, or can I just let the whole thing evaporate?"

Sunny laughs. "Good use of science in this conversation! But I don't know. Maybe just end it, so you're not stressing about it anymore? Enough is enough."

"I think you're right."

"Oh! I totally forgot to tell you!" Sunny says, right before I'm about to hang up.

"What? What?"

"Okay, so remember how you were obsessed with those old medicine bottles in the basement of the pharmacy?" she asks. "So, Evan went to this crafts fair in the Berkshires last weekend when he was visiting his grandma, and he was telling me all about this cool thing where people, like, put questions in medicine bottles, and other people put in pieces of advice or something."

"Huh?"

"Call Evan. He'll be able to explain it," she says. "I think it would be a cool addition to Eighth-Grade Masquerade."

"Thanks, I'll ask Evan."

I leave Evan a voice mail, but he doesn't call back. I really have no idea what Sunny's talking about, but I figure I'll find out soon enough.

I spend the rest of the night figuring out how to tell Travis. Obviously a text is too impersonal and mean. Maybe an e-mail? A phone call is probably better. Or I guess in person. Maybe I just need to tell him to meet me by my locker before first period, and we'll walk somewhere and I'll tell him. That's probably the simplest way to do it.

Hey Travis. Meet me by my locker before 1st period tomorrow. Okay? Goodnight.

After I send it, I immediately feel better. I'm taking a step in the right direction. The Travis thing was a fun experiment, but maybe he's not the right boy for me. Or maybe it's just not the right time. I need to get over Yamir before I can like anyone else.

A few minutes later, he texts back.

OK. Sweet dreams.

So he has no idea what's about to happen. Maybe boys really are clueless. I don't want to hurt him, but truthfully I bet there's a line of girls in our grade who'd want to go out with him. He's cute, and he has a planetarium in his house. I'm sure he'll find someone who likes him more than I do.

I toss and turn all night. It's not the Travis thing I'm worried about. I also need to figure out my costume. And I'm stressed about the spa. I know Penelope has it all under control, but things could go wrong.

I want everything about this to be perfect.

My grandma told me that Albert Einstein once said that insanity is doing the same thing over and over again and expecting different results. I'm basically doing that this year. Trying for a perfect last semester, trying to make things perfect for the AGE girls, trying to make the Masquerade perfect.

And I'm insane. There is no perfect. Things can never be perfect.

And what does perfect even mean? One person's perfect isn't the same as another person's perfect.

I need to accept that and move on. Maybe life isn't meant to be perfect. It's meant to be complicated and messy and confusing, and that's what makes it exciting and memorable. I mean, things with Erica Crane have always been up and down—and while it's been a lot of down, it's certainly been interesting. And the whole thing with Travis: it's not ideal, and I may be breaking his heart pretty soon, but the experience has taught me that even if someone likes you, you might not like them, and you can't really force yourself to. Lots of things in life are far from perfect, but maybe that's okay. Maybe we learn things from the imperfections.

Maybe perfect is really just another word for boring.

I needed all these things to happen—heartbreak with Yamir, Erica telling everyone my secrets, Claudia coming home to ask us for advice, ups and downs with Sunny—to make me realize this.

There is no perfect. There's only hoping for the best. And rolling with the punches.

That's it.

I get to school the next morning and Travis is waiting for me by my locker. He's wearing baggy army-green cargo pants and a long-sleeved navy T-shirt. He looks so cute. I wish he didn't look so cute.

"What's up?" he asks, still leaning against my locker, like a boy in some back-to-school clothing ad.

"Let's walk," I say, after my coat and books are put away. I take my bag and the books I'll need for the first few periods.

We walk up to the steps to the second-floor bathroom, but

obviously he can't go in there; it's a girls' room. So we walk farther down the hall until we find an empty classroom. I think it's used for the Mandarin class, and the Mandarin teacher doesn't come until fifth period.

We go inside and sit down at the desks. He slicks his hair back but it's all disheveled, and I immediately wonder if I'm making the wrong decision. Travis is cute. He's boring, but still cute.

"Talk to me, Desberg." Calling me by my last name—I love that, for some unknown reason. I've always loved it. Now what should I do? I have no idea.

"So, you heard about the 'no dates to the Masquerade' thing, right?" I ask. "I'm really glad the whole executive committee agreed. This way no one feels bad."

"I didn't hear that," he says. "But okay."

"So, like, we're not going as a couple," I say, trying to rephrase what I just said. Some part of me thinks he's not getting what I'm saying.

"Yeah, whatever." He raises his eyebrows. "That's fine. I'm doing some costume theme with my boys."

"Your boys?"

"Yeah. Gavin, Evan, Nicolai, Carmine, maybe even Luke if he can get his act together."

"Oh." So Travis wasn't even really concerned about going

with me. He wasn't worried about a costume theme with me. And he hasn't asked me to hang out in a few days. Maybe we've already broken up. Maybe I can just let things cool off naturally.

"So that's all you wanted to tell me?" he asks. He seems anxious to go. He keeps looking at the big clock above the door. That must be it: he knows what's up. That we're just not compatible, but he doesn't want to openly break it off either.

We're good. We're on the same page.

"That was it," I say.

"Cool. I gotta run and talk to Mr. D-H before class. He was not pleased with my essay on *The Outsiders*."

"Good luck with that." I smile. He doesn't ask me to walk with him, and he doesn't grab my hand or even try a little kiss before he goes.

I'm relieved. Everything is working out.

33

Lucy's tip for surviving eighth grade:
Don't assume you know how others feel.

Word about the no-dates plan spreads like wildfire throughout the eighth grade. Everyone is psyched about it—which is kind of surprising. All this year I thought people were in a rush to grow up and act like they're in high school. But they're not. Everyone just wants to hang out with their friends, and maybe talk about boys, or talk about girls. But nothing too serious.

It's refreshing.

Of course, it took Erica Crane's heartbreak to make this happen. And she'll probably never know the good deed she did. But maybe that's okay too. If she knew, it would go to her head.

I spend the rest of the day feeling pretty great. I'm off the hook with Travis, and everyone's excited that no one's going with a date. I even get an e-mail from Clint's dad about how thrilled everyone is with the vendors I found for the green cafeteria, and how if I want a job in Old Mill Schools Dining Services when I'm older, I'm hired.

I told him I'll keep it in mind. I think I'd be much happier as a makeup artist or a spa consultant, but you never know. This year is proof that everything can change—ideas, plans, aspirations. Being able to roll with it is what's most important.

Mrs. Deleccio and another science teacher have taken my composting idea and are handling it themselves. I'm so disappointed that I couldn't find time to do it. But I'm still glad I suggested it. Sometimes you really can't do it all. And I guess realizing that is more important than trying to do everything and completely freaking out and letting people down.

Sunny comes over after school to hammer out our costume plan. The AGE girls are going as oldies singers, like in "The Shoop Shoop Song." Annabelle's mom is really good at sewing, and she's making them poodle skirts and everything. They told me they have the "pink" part of the theme covered.

Apparently Travis and "his boys" are going as some kind of toe fungus. On his way to lunch he said, "We're gonna rock the green. Believe me."

It sounds completely disgusting, but whatever. I'm not planning on spending that much time with him anyway.

"Did you ever talk to Evan about the medicine bottles?" Sunny asks me. She's been going on and on about the grossness of what Evan's planning on wearing and how she's not going to be able to look at him.

"No. I left him a voice mail and then figured we'd talk in school, but we haven't had a chance," I say. To be honest, I'd totally forgotten about it.

"Oh. He never checks voice mail." Sunny shakes her head. She hops off my bed and goes to grab her bag off my window seat. When she gets back, she hands me her phone. "Call him."

"Now?"

He answers on the first ring, and I feel a little silly calling Sunny's boyfriend when she's sitting right here.

"Lucy!" He pauses and crunches some chips or pretzels or something. "I'm so glad you called again. I have to tell you about this thing I saw in the Berkshires."

"Yeah? Tell!"

He starts by telling me about a crafts fair he went to with his grandma and how one booth had a table of all these old medicine bottles. "It seems like the same thing you found in the basement of the pharmacy. But people would come up with questions or advice they needed. Like, one person wrote, 'How will I survive winter?' and then another person answered with 'Stand in direct sunlight, even when it's cold.'"

"Cool, but I don't really get it," I say.

He explains how the questions were taped to the bottles,

and people wrote advice on little slips of paper and put them inside the bottles.

"Sometimes it was a little hard to see the answers, so you'd have to shake the bottle a little," he says. "It was just a cool, crafty kind of thing. It seems like something you'd love. And then Sunny mentioned the bottles you found. And I thought it could be a good addition to the Masquerade."

"Oh!" I yelp, and Sunny startles. "I love that! We can have an advice booth. I can bring all the bottles from the pharmacy!"

"Exactly!"

Evan and I hang up, and I'm overcome with appreciation. Evan thought of this amazing idea, and it incorporates something from Old Mill Pharmacy. And all because Sunny remembered the medicine bottles.

"So what should we do for our costumes, though?" Sunny asks me after we've stopped discussing the medicine bottle idea.

"The Pink Ladies!" I exclaim. "From *Grease!*"

"Yeah?" Sunny doesn't seem thrilled.

"I mean, it fits the whole pink theme so well! And we love *Grease*. We know all the songs by heart." I pause to let it sink in. "It'll be like a tribute to our friendship."

"Well, when you put it that way . . ." Sunny smiles. "But we might need more than just the two of us to really pull it off. And is it too similar to the 'Shoop Shoop girls'?"

"It's similar in that we can hang out with them and it'll be cool. But not too similar, like we stole their idea," I say, and then something occurs to me. "We should ask Zoe and Erica if they want to do it too."

"Do you have the flu? You're asking *Erica Crane* to dress up with us?"

I plop down on the bed next to her. "Things have changed, Sun. We're almost in high school. Erica even sits at our lunch table now. She'll never be nice, but she'll always be here, so there's nothing we can do about it."

"Wait." Sunny furiously hits my knee. "Isn't Zoe's mom some kind of fashion consultant? I bet she'd be able to find us the most amazing costumes ever."

"Yes!" I high-five her.

We set up a second-floor-bathroom meeting with Erica and Zoe for the next morning. I hope that they're into this idea. It'll be awesome to have Zoe in our group, because I know her mom will make sure we have the most amazing costumes in the grade. But it's not only that. After all we've been through, it makes sense for us to be in a group with Erica and Zoe. It will symbolize a changing of the times, a new order of things.

We're growing up. We're nicer to each other now. Just because we spent the past seven years as enemies doesn't mean we can't spend the next four years as sort-of friends.

34

Lucy's tip for surviving eighth grade:

Always aim to be inclusive.

"So this is our idea," I tell Zoe and Erica in the second-floor bathroom the next morning. "Making sure we stay in line with Erica's awesome idea for the Pink and Green theme of the Masquerade, I think we should be the Pink Ladies."

"What?" Erica asks. I can tell she's in a bad mood. She still has her sunglasses on.

"Like from *Grease*," Sunny explains. "Lucy and I have been obsessed with *Grease* since, like, second grade, when my mom kind of didn't want us to watch it."

"Why not?" Erica asks.

"That doesn't really matter now," Sunny says. "But the costumes for the Pink Ladies are great. We'll obviously be very pink. And we can get fabulous fifties makeup to go along with it."

"I like it," Zoe says, looking to Erica for approval. I bet

every night, Zoe has to text Erica a picture of the outfit she plans to wear the next day. Or maybe they just video-chat the night before.

"It sounds okay," Erica says. "Honestly, I don't really even care anymore. This whole thing has been exhausting."

"So it's a yes?" I yelp. "Yay! This is gonna be awesome!"

We all ignore Erica's negative attitude and move forward with our plans. I bring up how we could shop for costumes online or at thrift stores, and then Zoe says, "No, no. no. My mom has, like, fifty closets full of clothes she's used for shoots and stuff. We'll look there. And if not, she can call one of her people. They'll hook us up."

"That is so amazing," Sunny says. "Thank you!"

"Yup. Trust me. We're gonna look fabulous."

Erica groans, "Whatever," and we all leave the bathroom.

We have about a week to get the costumes in order, but that seems like enough time. It's all coming together.

When I get home from school, Yamir is sitting on my front porch. At first I think my eyes are playing tricks on me. But no, he's really there. He's wearing his big navy winter coat. He has his hood up and his gloves on, but he still looks like he's freezing. Who knows how long he's been out here. Mom and Grandma are at the pharmacy late these days, taking care of the new shipments and hiring a few backup pharmacists so they can take more time off.

"I thought you'd never come home," he says as soon as he sees me.

I look at my watch. "School just got out twenty minutes ago. I got a ride home from Zoe's mom, so that's why I'm here so early."

"Oh. I forgot. High school ends at 2:26."

"That's a very exact time." I sit down on the rocking chair next to him.

"Aren't you wondering why I'm here?" He looks at me, but I don't look at him. I can't, for some reason. Maybe it's because I still don't believe he's really here, sitting on my porch, sitting next to me.

I nod.

"What happened with us, Luce-Juice?" he asks in the softest, sweetest voice I've ever heard him use.

"You really need to ask that?" I finally look at him.

"Yeah."

Are boys born with only half the brain that girls are born with? Does it grow over time? I don't understand how he doesn't get it.

"Yamir, you ignored me for weeks."

"I was busy."

"So then tell me you're busy," I say, as matter-of-fact as can be. "Don't just ignore me."

"It seems like the kind of thing you'd figure out. Like, why would I just ignore you for no reason?"

"I thought you didn't like me anymore."

"Why would I just stop liking you?" he looks at me again and I look at him, and I think he has been genuinely confused this whole time. "You're Lucy."

"I know who I am." I didn't mean for that to come out rude, but I'm not sure what to say. He needs to know it's not cool to just ignore someone. And then it dawns on me. What if I'm doing that same exact thing with Travis? Ignoring him until he gets tired of it? I need to make sure I'm not.

"Well, I still think about you," he says. "I mean, I've been sitting out here freezing for forty-five minutes."

"Sorry about that," I say.

"I still think about you a lot." He inches his rocking chair closer to mine and nudges me with his shoulder.

"That's good to know. But I think I also deserve an apology." He can't go around thinking he can behave any way he wants and that I'll always just be here waiting. I wouldn't be able to respect myself if I acted like that.

"I deserve an apology too," he says. "You and that Travis kid? Come on."

"What?"

"Oh, don't *what* me. You were totally spending time with him, when I thought we were still together."

"How can we be together if we don't talk for weeks and weeks?" I huff. This is exhausting.

"We're going around in circles, Luce-Juice." He smiles a little, but I don't. I don't find any of this funny.

"Well, we obviously disagree. So let's just talk about it another time." I stand up. "You can come in if you need to warm up."

"That's okay," he says to my back. "I'll just see you around."

I go inside and replay that conversation over and over in my head. It's good to know he thinks about me, but until he realizes what he did wrong, we can never work.

I used to think that Yamir could read my mind and know exactly how I was feeling. But maybe I shouldn't expect that. Clearly he's not getting it. Maybe one day he will. But for now, I need to accept that Lucy and Yamir are two individual people, doing our own things, apart from each other.

It doesn't matter what we used to be. We aren't that way anymore.

35

Lucy's tip for surviving eighth grade:
Be appreciative when others do for you.

With only two days to go until the Masquerade, Sunny and I go to Zoe's house to try on our costumes. In a way it feels like I've been waiting forever for this, and in another way it feels like it just snuck up on me.

"So, you girls like the costumes?" Zoe's mom asks. She's wearing skinny jeans and a button-down shirt. I bet she was a model back in the day.

"Oh yeah. Amazing," I answer. "How did you pull this off so quickly?"

"Let's just say I have connections." She winks.

We all have the signature pink jackets with the words "Pink Ladies" written on the back. We'll wear black leggings underneath, with a black T-shirt, and we'll get our hair and makeup done to match the girls in *Grease*.

"We look so awesome," Erica says. "I can't even believe it!"

"I can believe it!" I shriek. "We're hot."

Everyone bursts out laughing, and it feels like we're in some kind of alternate universe. Sunny and I having fun with Erica Crane—how did we get here? I don't even know.

We're parading in front of Zoe's full-length mirror with our Pink Ladies jackets on when Zoe's phone starts ringing, to the melody of a Taylor Swift song.

"Who is it?" Erica asks. She always needs to know who's calling, even when it's not her phone. It's kind of an obsession.

"Gavin," Zoe says. "Hey, Gav," she says into the phone. "What's up?"

Gav? Is she for real?

Erica huffs and walks into Zoe's bathroom and closes the door. I guess she's annoyed that Zoe has a boyfriend and she doesn't. Who knows. I can't dwell on it. We have the costumes we wanted, and we already agreed that no one is bringing a date. All I need is for things to go smoothly at the spa on the day of the event, and I'll be happy.

Well, as happy as I can be without Yamir.

"Just trying on our costumes," Zoe says. "Me, Erica, Lucy, and Sunny."

Zoe looks at me and then turns away. "Yeah, Lucy's here."

Uh-oh. I don't even know what they're talking about, but I don't like the sound of it.

"Sure, yeah. Come over. We'll order pizza or something."

Oh no. Now I know I don't like the sound of it.

"Yeah, bring Evan too." She pauses. "He does? Oh, fab. She'll be so psyched."

Zoe hangs up, and all I can think about is finding some kind of escape route out of here.

"Sunny," I whisper while Zoe goes to get Erica out of her bathroom. "Do you know what's going on?"

"No. Evan said he had to help his mom clean out the basement." She shrugs. "But don't worry. We'll just hang out in a group."

Sunny's looking at her phone, not paying attention to me.

Erica and Zoe come out of the bathroom. Erica's been crying and she smells like Zoe's fancy perfume. I'm not sure the two things go together, but at least she smells nice.

"You're never going to believe this," Erica says.

Sunny and I look up.

"Hunter Adelson is coming over here. Right now."

"What?" I ask. Hunter's one of those boys in our grade who everyone has a secret crush on. He's always been nice and cute and smart. He's like the perfect boy, basically, but he never goes out with anyone. He just does his own thing.

"You heard me," Erica says. "He's been hanging out with Gavin. And he's coming here now. Zoe says he likes me."

"Really?" I ask, trying to hide the shock in my voice. Clearly this is bad news. Now is not the time for anyone to like Erica. She'll try to revoke our no-dates plan. And Hunter Adelson? He can't really like Erica. Has he lost his mind? I mean, she's nicer now, sure, but she's not that nice.

"Yup," Zoe says. "Lucy, come into my bathroom. I need to show you this blush."

Something seriously weird is going on, but I follow Zoe into the bathroom. She closes the door, and I feel bad that Sunny's left in Zoe's room alone with Erica.

"Okay, so Hunter doesn't really *like* like Erica. I mean, he doesn't dislike her. But the thing is, she's been so down. And all the other boys are coming over. You, me, and Sunny have boyfriends, and she doesn't. So Gavin said he'd bring Hunter, and I may have just told a white lie. But *shh*. We're all just gonna hang out together anyway. What difference does it make?"

We hear Sunny yell, "What's going on in there?" and I know that this day is going to deteriorate fast. First, I need to make sure Travis knows he's not my boyfriend. Second, I'm scared about what Erica's going to do to Hunter Adelson. Or to Zoe, when she figures out that Zoe made up the whole thing.

"Let's go," I say.

"Do you understand?" Zoe puts her hands on my shoulders, looking serious and kind of scary. "Just go with it, okay?"

I almost tell her that I pretty much broke up with Travis the other day, but then Erica starts complaining about her outfit and how she needs to borrow a skirt of Zoe's, and Zoe gets all panicked and we leave the bathroom.

Things are going to be fine. I tell myself that over and over again. I wish all of this wasn't happening two days before the Masquerade, but it is, and I can deal with it.

Zoe's mom knocks on the door. "Zo, I have to run out and take care of a few things. You okay here? Dad should be home by seven."

"Oh yeah." Zoe smiles. "We're fine." She doesn't mention the group of four boys that's on the way here right now. Does her mom know? For some reason this secrecy makes me even more nervous.

When her mom leaves, Zoe closes the door and whispers, "I'm so glad you didn't say anything about the boys. My mom's cool, but not about stuff like that. She'd freak out if she knew they were all coming over. But I knew she was going out. And my dad always gets home late."

So clearly I had reason to be nervous.

Breathe, Lucy. Breathe. Travis was cool with everything. He didn't seem fazed or upset about it. So I have no idea why I'm freaking out right now.

36

Lucy's tip for surviving eighth grade:
Realize that even the worst times end eventually.

The boys arrive, and at first everything is fine. We go into Zoe's den and put on some old cartoon, and we're all just sitting on the couches hanging out and talking. Zoe brings in some soda and pita chips and hummus, and I start to calm down.

Everything is going to be fine.

But then, things change.

Sunny and Evan decide to "go for a walk," even though it's thirty degrees outside. Clearly they're not walking very far, probably just upstairs to the computer room to be alone. Sunny and Evan have been together so long that no one really pays attention to them. They're kind of like an old married couple, but a happy one.

Then Zoe tells Gavin she wants to show him the new giant TV in her basement, and they go downstairs. Now, all of this is pretty innocent. It's not like we're in some kind of cheesy high school movie where crazy stuff happens. It's just that everyone is disappearing to be alone with someone else— and I don't like it.

So then it's just Hunter, Erica, Travis, and me watching the cartoon and eating the pita chips. And it starts to get awkward. Erica keeps flipping her hair all around, and it's making me dizzy. It looks like it's making Hunter dizzy too, because he keeps squinting and backing away from her on the couch.

"Hunter, are you still really into the violin?" I ask. It sounds nerdy, but the thing is, Hunter plays some kind of rock violin. He travels to Providence for lessons, and he's really serious about it. He always gets a solo at the winter concert and then a standing ovation.

"Oh yeah. I think I'm starting a band with these kids from Madison in a few months," he tells me. "We have the same teacher, and we're pretty pumped about it."

"Sounds cool," I say. Hunter's one of those kids that's going to be famous one day.

"Hey, Hunter," Erica says, putting her hair up for the twentieth time. "Zoe's dad plays electric guitar. He has this whole music room upstairs. Come on, I'll show you."

This is my fault. I shouldn't have brought up the violin. But we were all just sitting there silently watching Erica do crazy things with her hair, and it was getting awkward. I even found a few strands of hair in the hummus. Gross.

"Cool," is all he says, and he follows her upstairs. It's too bad that Zoe's house has so much interesting stuff.

The cartoon is still on, and Travis seems pretty engrossed in it. And he's still eating the hummus. I'm not sure he realizes that everyone else has left the den.

"So, Travis," I start. It takes a few seconds for him to look up. And the longer I wait to say this, the harder it's going to be. I wasn't really honest the other day. If I've learned anything this year, it's that you have to open up.

"Yeah, what's up?" He looks at me, and I start to feel guilty about what I'm going to say. But I know it's the right thing.

"So . . . the other day when I brought up the whole no-dates thing. Um, I don't feel like I really said all I needed to say. The thing is, um, I don't know what you're thinking about the two of us, and stuff," I say. "But, like, I feel like we're just better as friends. And maybe you already knew that, but I just wanted to be honest." I pause. "Honesty's the best policy, you know?"

I feel like a total idiot for saying that last part, but I couldn't think of what else to say.

He's looking at the TV again. And then he says, "Wait, what? Sorry, I spaced."

He's really going to make me say this whole thing again?

"I was just saying that, like, I don't know what you're thinking about us. But I think we should just be friends." There. I said it. Sure, it's a little bit lame and the cliché you hear all the time. But it's true. He's nice for a friend. For a boyfriend, he's not for me.

"Oh. Um. Yeah, sure. Whatever." He looks at me for half a second and then stares at the TV again, shoving the rest of the pita chip crumbs into his mouth.

That's it? I wonder. I should feel relieved right now, but instead I just feel confused.

We sit there for what feels like forever. Travis is flipping through the channels on someone else's TV and drinking five cans of Dr Pepper. I play games on my phone and then text Claudia:

Ended things with Travis. Still weird with Yamir. Excited for Masquerade.

I get a quick reply:

Glad you're excited. All is well here. Frigid but good. Bean & I are going skiing this weekend. xoxo

We text back and forth a few more times. I watch the clock ticking above the doorway. This evening will end. Even the most boring, awkward evenings come to an end eventually.

Soon everyone comes back, Zoe orders a pizza, and we all sit around eating and laughing. I don't know if Hunter really likes Erica, but maybe it doesn't matter. She seems happy now, and he's not even paying that much attention to her. Maybe sometimes we just need to be told what we want to hear, even if it's not totally true. It's not lying exactly, just a little fib.

Like the whole thing with Claudia—I wonder if Mom and Grandma really would have forbidden her from marrying Bean. She's an adult; could they even do that? But I think hearing them say "no way" was what Claudia wanted to hear. She loves Bean and she's happy with him, but I think she was scared to think too much about getting married. She almost wanted them to forbid her. Even though it was a fake proposal with a Ring Pop for two years from now, she still got scared.

I guess Erica was scared too. Scared of everyone moving on to high school with boyfriends, maybe. Or scared of being all alone. It's hard to say.

So many things have surprised me this year. Some good surprises. Some bad surprises. I guess that's just the way life works sometimes. The more you feel like you have everything figured out, the less you actually do.

Lucy's tip for surviving eighth grade:
Try to slow down and enjoy the moment.

I wake up at five in the morning on the day of the Masquerade. I try as hard as I can to fall back asleep, but I can't. My mind is spinning with worry and excitement and is fizzy with anticipation.

I go downstairs and cuddle up under a blanket on the couch. Maybe if I turn on the TV, I'll drift back to sleep. But no. I'm up. I text Sunny to see if she's up too, but I don't get a response. She must still be sleeping.

When you wake up at five in the morning, you're starving. So I scramble up some eggs with cheese. I pop some slices of my favorite oatmeal bread into the toaster. I cut up strawberries and bananas and pour myself a tall glass of grapefruit juice. A breakfast fit for a queen. And as nervous as I am, I'm still able to eat all of it.

After breakfast, I go back upstairs, crawl into bed, and

start reading. And then I fall back asleep. I guess my body was so tired from all the eating that it just needed to rest again. When I wake up this time, it's eight, and I only have fifteen minutes to get to the spa before the first appointment.

Now I'm running late and I'm rushing, and the gourmet breakfast I ate is sitting in my stomach like a pile of wet laundry.

I pack my costume carefully in a bag and head downstairs, dressed in whatever sweatpants and sweatshirt were on my desk chair. They seem clean enough.

"You ready?" Mom asks as soon as she sees me. "I was worried you'd oversleep."

"I was up at five," I explain. "And then I fell back asleep."

"Ah, so that's where the frying pan in the sink came from. I thought we had middle-of-the-night intruders who like omelets."

"Nope. Only me."

"Dad's on his way to drive you to the spa," Mom says. "He wanted to make sure he saw you on your special day."

I take a minute to think about that, and appreciate it. All the years he lived in London, I never imagined he'd be back and living so close to me. That's the thing about life—you never really know what will change, and whether that change is good or bad. You have to be open to anything.

"Ready?" my dad asks me after I'm in the car.

"I think so." I smile. "Thanks for driving me."

I almost fall asleep on the short drive over to the spa. I'm so excited about this day, but I'm also really tired. I hope I can run on adrenaline. Ninety makeup treatments need to go smoothly, and then I need to have the best time ever at Eighth-Grade Masquerade. After everything that's happened, I'm still striving for perfection. I guess that's just the way I am.

And you're only in eighth grade once, after all.

38

Lucy's tip for surviving eighth grade:
Baked goods make a good thing even better.

At the spa, Penelope has set up the reception area with the most amazing spread: scones, muffins, cut-up fruit, fresh-squeezed juice, and Greek yogurt.

"I didn't want anyone to get hungry," Penelope explains. "And if we run out of seats, I set up the Relaxation Room as well."

I smile. I haven't heard anyone call it that in so long, but it's refreshing to hear. My idea. My creation. And it still exists. People still hang out there when they're waiting for their prescriptions.

"Great. Thank you so much!" I give Penelope a hug. "And thanks for getting up so early to make it here."

"Of course. This is your day. And it's going to be an amazing one."

I hope she's right. One doofy eighth-grade boy could ruin

242

the whole thing. I'm imagining someone like Matt getting a bloody nose all over the beautiful couches in here. He can't help it, some people say, but I think he can. I won't get into the reasons why. They're too disgusting. Or someone like Andy could sneak in and put on a face mask and walk around that way, making everyone laugh and wasting our products.

Middle school boys can be so dumb. I guess middle school girls can be dumb too, though—getting into fights, crying over everything, storming out of the room, refusing to talk to someone. I've been through it all over the past few years.

I guess we just have to hope for the best.

I told Erica, Zoe, and Sunny to get here early too, and they show up right on time. They come rushing in, all excited.

"Oh my God, it looks unbelievable in here," Erica says. "I'm too nervous to eat. Okay, actually, I can't resist." She takes a chocolate chip scone off the table.

Penelope takes us on a tour of all the treatment rooms. They're modified so that a few makeup applications can go on at the same time. Everything is set up perfectly, and I can't wait for everyone to get here.

"Here's the schedule, Lucy." Grace walks over to us. "I gave each person a half hour. That should be more than enough time. And I know not everyone in the grade signed up. So we can accommodate some walk-ins."

"Those people are dumb," Erica says. "They clearly don't know what they're missing."

People with early appointments start trickling in. Grace made sure that kids with complicated costumes come in early—like Luca Smith, who's getting some crazy Darth Vader thing done, or Blythe Silverstein, who literally wants her face to look like Taylor Swift's. I'm not exactly sure how Mary the makeup artist is going to make that happen. She's the best in the world, but that's still a little complicated. She's not a plastic surgeon, after all.

Zoe, Erica, Sunny, and I are getting our makeup done late in the day, because it isn't that complicated and we wanted it to be as fresh as possible. But we came early to oversee everything. I decided to leave the makeup work to the amazing spa staff, so I could enjoy the day without being too stressed.

Now groups of kids start to show up. The sporty boys like Phil, Sam, and Mark are getting some kind of wacky makeup that makes their skin look like leather.

Mina, Leslie, Angie, and all the other super-studious girls aren't getting much done, just a little eye shadow and blush. I think they're going as colors of the rainbow.

It's funny to see where people go with the whole "come up with your own costume" thing. Most people are following the Pink & Green theme, since Erica basically drilled it into their heads. She reminded the whole grade every day at lunch and put up posters and had all the homeroom teachers remind everyone too. She's a drill sergeant, but this Masquerade was her big thing and she wants it to go perfectly. I get that.

The AGE girls come in a little after that, all psyched about their "Shoop Shoop girls" theme. They even have images printed out from the Internet of what they want their makeup to look like.

"I am *so so so so so* excited," Annabelle tells me. "I never could have imagined how awesome this would be."

"Yay! That's so great!"

"And you don't know how happy everyone is that we're all going stag. No dates to worry about. Just fun with your friends."

"Exactly." I smile.

"I mean, if Owen McDonald asks me to dance, I won't say no," she whispers. "I've basically been in love with him since first grade."

"Really? I didn't know that." I widen my eyes. Annabelle thinks she's revealing a secret, but I think everyone in the entire world knows.

Around noon, the spa is bursting with people. Even the kids who've already had their makeup done hang out and eat and talk with everyone. It's like there's a pre-party going on right here.

I walk around and peek into all the treatment rooms. Everyone seems pleased and looks fabulous. Then I go to the Relaxation Room. Sunny, Zoe, and Erica are sitting on one of the couches in the corner, whispering about something. As soon as they see me, they stop talking. What's that about?

I hope they're not planning some elaborate prank. But Sunny wouldn't do that to me. At least I don't think she would.

"I gotta go meet Evan," Sunny says. "The 'toe fungus boys' should be arriving any minute." She sticks her tongue out, pretending she's about to throw up.

"Yeah, Suzanne the makeup artist was really pumped about that one," I say. "But she used to do makeup for Broadway shows, so she's prepared. That's why Grace assigned her to Evan and the boys."

"Good thinking." Sunny pats me on the shoulder and walks away.

"Toe fungus costume or not, Gavin is still going to look so cute," Zoe says. She looks at Erica. "I know, no dates, no dates. But whatever, we're still going to dance. I mean, that's okay, right?"

Erica shrugs. "I guess."

"And we're totally kissing at the end of the night," Zoe says. "I know we are. It hasn't happened yet. But it will."

"Whatever you say, Zo." Erica rolls her eyes at me. "Keep dreaming."

Erica is so mean to Zoe, and Zoe just takes it. I don't really get their friendship. I probably never will.

"If you want to kiss a toe fungus, be my guest." Erica falls back into the couch, cracking up.

"Oh, and Elias was *soooo* much better." Zoe glares at Erica. "I mean, aren't you the one who told me he had to ride backward in a car seat until he was, like, six years old?"

"Yeah. So?"

"And his mom was still bringing him homemade fruit puree in elementary school. Like he didn't even have teeth!"

"That's his mom," Erica defends. "But it doesn't matter. We're over anyway."

"You're lucky you got out now," Zoe says. "He was definitely weird. Remember that day he said he wondered how many toenail clippings it would take to fill up a whole room?"

"I'm tired of talking about this. It's boring," Erica says. "Good luck with kissing Gavin. We can all find boys to kiss if we want to. It's just that none of them are worthy of me."

I pat Erica on the back. "Okay, let's go back to the spa," I say.

"Oh, you're in such a rush to see Travis?" Erica asks me. "Now that you've broken his heart."

"I did not. He didn't even care. We're on good terms."

To be honest, I'd totally forgotten about him. Even with all the talk about Gavin and Evan and the fungal infection costumes.

"Whatever you say," Erica adds.

We all leave the pharmacy and walk into the spa.

It occurs to me that when you're busy thinking about your friends, you don't have much time to think about boys. Maybe it's better that way.

39

Lucy's tip for surviving eighth grade:
Compliment others.

ᘓach makeup treatment is better than the one before it, and the day flies by. Everyone is thrilled with how they look.

Soon parents are coming to pick up their kids and take them over to school for the Masquerade. A lot of the kids brought costumes and changed at the spa, so Mom and Grandma take pictures of everyone and e-mail them out right away.

We get to school, and there's a giant banner on the building that reads EIGHTH-GRADE MASQUERADE: PINK & GREEN IS THE NEW BLACK.

"You made that sign?" I ask Erica as we're walking in.

"Well, Sunny helped. Her dad too."

"Ramal Printing's finest!" Sunny laughs.

We walk inside, and the gym is decorated like I've never

seen before—balloons and streamers and tables with pink-and-green polka-dot tablecloths.

"You did all of this?" I turn to Erica and Zoe.

"We did. Our labor of love," Zoe says.

We walk over to admire the table that's set up with all the old medicine bottles and little slips of paper for advice seekers and advice givers.

"I love this idea," Zoe says. "I'm so glad you thought of it."

"It was all Evan," I tell them. "I mean, I had the bottles; I found them in the basement of the pharmacy. But it was his idea. He saw it at a crafts fair." I go on and on about this because it proves one very important thing: sometimes boys can be very helpful.

The teachers are wearing either all pink or all green, and they look great. People come in and the DJ starts playing music—everything from the Beatles to Justin Timberlake—and everyone is dancing.

I look around at my class and I can't believe this is it. Our Eighth-Grade Masquerade is here.

And soon it will be over. In a few months we'll all be moving on from Old Mill Middle School. We'll be leaving behind the disgusting tuna sandwiches. And Mrs. Deleccio and Earth Club. We'll be going to Old Mill High School with kids we don't know—kids from Waterside Middle School and Strat-field Middle School.

"Having fun?" Sunny asks, putting her arm around me.

"Yeah. Just taking it all in."

"Pretty great, right?"

"Where's your 'toe fungus boy'?" I ask her, and laugh.

"Who knows," she says. "You know, having a boyfriend isn't all it's cracked up to be."

"It's not?" I ask.

"I mean, it's great sometimes. But you know how everyone looked at you like your life was perfect just because you had a boyfriend? That whole thing kind of annoys me. It's really fun and all, but it doesn't mean everything is perfect in your life all the time. I mean, I still worry about my grandma getting older, and how many times I'll get to see her since she lives in India. I worry about grades and tests. Life isn't perfect just because you have a boyfriend."

"True."

To be honest, I wasn't even thinking that much about having a boyfriend. I was thinking about how grateful I am that Erica Crane turned a tiny drop nicer, that I stopped worrying about grown-up problems, and that I had time to focus on eighth-grade problems.

Maybe things aren't perfect, or how I imagined they'd be. But they're still pretty great.

"Travis keeps staring at you, by the way."

"He does not," I declare, because I really want it to be true.

"He does." She points over to where he's standing. "Poor kid."

"Oh, he's fine," I tell her. "Half the girls here would be happy to dance with him."

"If the DJ ever plays a slow song," Sunny says. "Maybe Erica gave him specific instructions not to."

"Very possible," I say.

We walk over to the drinks table and pour ourselves glasses of strawberry punch.

Mr. Marblane stands up on the temporary stage and thanks everyone for all their hard work. He brings Erica up, and everyone applauds her and she curtsies. It's clear she was waiting for this, and she's enjoying every second. And she deserves it. It's a great dance.

Then Mr. Marblane thanks Pink & Green: The Spa at Old Mill Pharmacy for all the awesome makeup work, and he thanks me for coordinating it. He thanks Sunny and Ramal Printing for the great sign. And then he tells everyone to go back to having fun and to continue behaving.

And then the DJ finally puts on a slow song, and Travis walks over to me, and I want to sink into the floor.

40

Lucy's tip for surviving eighth grade:
Dance even when you feel awkward about it.

"**Will you dance with me?**" Travis asks. The green makeup is piled on his face like clumpy mashed potatoes.

"Um." I will myself to say yes. It's just a dance. "Sure."

I put my arms around his neck, and he puts his arms around my waist. He smells like the strawberry punch he's been drinking all night. Clumps of makeup are falling off his face and landing on his shoulders. I think it's because he's sweating so much. The makeup is literally melting off his face.

"Sorry things got so weird between us," he says. I want to tell him that they didn't get weird. That there's really no us. That sometimes one person likes another person, but that other person doesn't like them back. It's a fact of life.

"They're not that weird," I say. I guess he was actually paying attention all those times I tried to talk to him about us. We're swaying back and forth, and I force myself to look him in the eyes and not look around to see who everyone else is dancing with. I pray that Gavin asked Zoe to dance, and that Erica didn't ruin it for them.

"I still like you, Lucy," Travis says. Oh no. That's not what I wanted to hear. I thought we were done with this.

"That's nice, Travis." I smile. "I just think I have to do my own thing for a while."

Oh Lord. What am I saying?

"You can do your own thing. I'll give you space," he says. "I mean, I just like hanging out with you. And summer is coming soon. And remember when we first met, and you told me how awesome summer in Old Mill is?"

I nod.

"I want to hang with you during the awesome time. When we don't have to worry about school or anything." He pauses and leans toward me and—oh no, he's going for a kiss. Not here. Not here. *Please* not here. But then he pulls back. My heart is still pounding. "Just think about it."

"Okay. Well, summer is still a while away." I pause for a second. It's hard to take him seriously with the green and brown blobs all over his face. "I'll think about it."

The song ends and we pull apart, and Travis says, "See ya, Lucy," as if he's leaving the dance for good.

I stand there, watching him walk away, wondering why I

can't just like him. But I can't. You can't force yourself to like someone. It just doesn't work that way.

"Did you see? Did you see?" Zoe asks, all out of breath, falling into me.

"No! What? Tell!"

"You didn't see Gavin and me dancing? For real?"

"Sorry," I say. "Was it awesome?"

"Yes, beyond." She smiles, still out of breath. "I hope there are more slow songs coming up."

"That's great, Zo." I high-five her. "I'm really happy for you."

It feels good to be happy for someone else even when you're not all-around happy in the same category yourself. Like, she has a boy that she likes that probably likes her, and even though I don't have that, I'm excited for her.

That's what being a true friend is all about, I think. That's what Erica still needs to work on. But maybe she's the kind of person who won't ever realize that. I guess we'll have to wait and see.

The Masquerade continues. There are more slow dances, but Travis doesn't ask me again. No one else does either. It's okay, though. Erica and I sway together during one. And then I do a little group dance with the AGE girls during another.

I go over to the medicine bottle table and check out the

anonymous advice seekers. I shake the bottles a little so I can see the answers.

Someone wrote: How can I be more outgoing? And someone else answered: Smile and try to say hi to one new person each day.

Good advice.

Another person wrote: Any idea how I can get my parents to understand me?

The answer: Say what's on your mind. And then be ready to listen.

Good questions and great answers. And the best part is, it's all anonymous.

It's such a simple touch, but it's never been done before for Eighth-Grade Masquerade. It's unique. It's us. And that's what makes it so special.

Finally it's time for the presentation part of the event. Mr. Marblane calls every group and individual onto the stage, one at a time, and we all go up and show off our costumes. It's cheesy, but fun anyway. It's really what the Masquerade is all about. It's not about a theme, though that's fun. And it's not about who is going with who. It's about showing ourselves off to one another. Being proud of who we are. Maybe it's because we'll all be moving on soon and we'll want to remember everyone as we were in eighth grade. Maybe it's because all these years we never took the time to really get to know each other or see each other. We just relied on old ideas we had of each other.

But the thing is, people can change. People do change. Erica Crane is living proof of that. Even a little change is still a change. Sure, she's never going to be a nice person. And I'm not even sure I want to be her friend. But she has changed a tiny, tiny bit.

And when I think back to how I was when I started at Old Mill Middle School—wow! I've really changed. I mean, the whole thing about Earth Club was a huge change. I didn't even want to join, and look what I've accomplished: the grant for the pharmacy, an eco-spa, a green cafeteria. It's pretty unbelievable. And I guess my worrying has changed a little too. I still worry—about grown-up problems, about thirteen-year-old problems—but it's different. The worrying doesn't take up all my time anymore.

People do change. We all change. I guess when you think about it, that's all life really is—a series of changes. Change after change after change. And all we can do is be ready and open for them.

It took a Masquerade and costumes to realize it. Visual proof of change, and a moment to shine.

It was all right there in front of us. But it took a night like this for us to realize it.

41

Lucy's tip for surviving eighth grade:
Really listen to others when they talk to you. Don't just wait to talk back.

The dance winds down and people start to trickle out. Evan and Sunny are sitting at a table in the corner, talking close, and I don't want to get too near them and ruin their moment. The rest of the "toe fungus boys" are playing some doofy game where they try to hit a balled-up napkin with a paper plate.

"Hello? The environment. The whole green part of the theme?" I frown at them. "Stop wasting paper goods."

"They're made from recycled materials," Gavin tells me, like I don't already know. "It says so right here."

"Duh. I know. I picked all the stuff. But you still shouldn't waste it," I tell them.

"Lucy's the Lorax, don't you know that?" we hear someone say. The voice is coming from behind us, so we all turn around.

I'd know the voice anywhere. It's Yamir.

No one says anything. Travis turns away and walks toward the snack table, pretending he's searching for the best chunk of cubed cheese.

The other boys scatter, and soon Yamir and I are just standing there, in the Old Mill Middle School gym.

He's not in a costume. Why would he be? But it seems funny to see someone in regular clothes around the rest of us in pink and green. He's wearing his skinny jeans and a gray collared sweater. He looks older. Well, older than he usually does, I guess. His hair isn't disheveled or shaggy. It's short and neat, like he's on his way to some important dinner.

"You are, you know," he says, softly.

"I'm what?"

"The Lorax. You speak for the trees."

I smile. "I guess there are worse things to be."

He nods. "Can we talk? Outside, maybe?"

"Sure," I reply.

I look around. Sunny and Evan are still in the corner. Zoe and Erica are on the stage, dancing to music streaming from Zoe's iPhone. The DJ has pretty much packed up, but I guess they still want to dance. There are teachers milling about, but no one is kicking us out yet.

"Why is he here?" Erica says, loud enough for the whole gym to stop what they're doing and look around.

I ignore her. I've spent too much time thinking about Erica Crane—wondering if she's changed, hoping I can trust her. But the truth is, I don't need to be friends with everyone. Some people will never be close. Maybe that's something that everyone needs to learn sooner or later.

No one else seems to notice that Yamir is here, or that we're walking out of the gym. Zoe's mom is supposed to pick us up, and then we're all sleeping at her house. I hope they don't leave without me. But I guess I can always find a way there.

It's a warm March night, and I realize I'm okay without a coat. That's a good thing, since I left it on the rack outside the gym, and I don't really want to go in and get it. This Pink Ladies jacket is surprisingly warm.

Yamir and I sit down on the curb outside the school. There are a million stars, and if I breathe in as hard as I can, I'm almost able to smell the ocean.

"I'm sorry," he says. "I'm so sorry."

I look at him. Yamir is sitting next to me, apologizing.

"I know I was an idiot. I know I ignored you. I don't know why I did it."

I keep looking at him. I want him to talk more. I don't want to interrupt his train of thought. I want him to speak his mind, to tell me everything. I want him to talk forever.

"I guess I was scared. Scared that I would totally mess up, and there would be no way to fix it, and you'd hate me forever. Also, I have to admit—I was kinda scared I'd have no time for my friends," he tells me. "This isn't an excuse. I'm just trying to explain myself."

I nod, willing him to continue.

"And as I was doing it, I knew it was dumb. And I wanted to explain myself. But then I thought you'd be mad. And so I just kept ignoring and being weird, and then I got used to it. And I convinced myself it was fine." He looks at me. "But the whole time I really missed you. And I wanted to talk to you. It was like I was torturing myself for no reason."

"That's really dumb," I say. "No offense."

He starts laughing, and then I start laughing. But it's not really all that funny. It's just a little overwhelming that he's saying all of this. That he's admitting he was wrong and saying he's sorry. I knew he had it in him. It just took a little while for him to open up.

"Anyway, I'm sorry. One hundred percent sorry. And I couldn't wait another day to tell you that."

"So you showed up at Eighth-Grade Masquerade?" I ask. "I think it's really because you missed middle school so much."

"Well, yeah. That too." He smiles.

"I knew it."

"I checked with Sunny. And she seemed to think it was okay. If I came at the end, when everything was over."

"She's smart."

"Yes, she got the smarts in the family. I got the looks."

We stay on the curb for a few more minutes, looking at the stars and laughing about things that probably aren't so funny. Right now, everything looks beautiful. Even the Old Mill Middle School parking lot looks landscaped and perfect.

"Can you forgive me?" Yamir asks, finally.

"I guess."

"You guess?"

"Well, I didn't expect this. It's catching me a little off guard."

"You didn't expect me coming here?" he asks. "Or you didn't expect that I'd apologize?"

"I didn't expect any of it. To be honest, I figured we were done. Like, actually done. Every story has an ending."

"Come on." He looks at me and gives me the tiniest, smallest, littlest peck on the lips. I think that catches me off guard more than him showing up, or this conversation, or anything else. "We're Lucy and Yamir. Our story is whatever we want it to be. But I don't think it's done."

"Okay." I smile. "I'll trust you on that."

"We're just getting to the good part." He stands up, and takes my hand, and we walk back inside.

The good part. I hear his voice in my head.

We'll go to high school and things will change. That's for sure. But we're just getting to the good part.

Acknowledgments

My sincerest thanks to Maggie Lehrman and everyone at Abrams and Amulet who believed in Lucy from the start and helped bring her story to life.

And to all the readers who have enjoyed Lucy's story—thank you, thank you, thank you from the bottom of my heart.

About the Author

Lisa Greenwald is the author of *Welcome to Dog Beach, Reel Life Starring Us, Sweet Treats & Secret Crushes,* and the Pink & Green series. She works in the library at the Birch Wathen Lenox School in Manhattan. She is a graduate of The New School's MFA program in writing for children and lives in Brooklyn. Visit her online at lisagreenwald.com.